Also by Stuart Woods
Available from Random House Large Print

Bombshell
Hit List

CHOPPY WATER

STUART WOODS

CHOPPY WATER

Copyright © 2020 by Stuart Woods

Published in the United States of America by Random House Large Print in association with G. P. Putnam's Sons, an imprint of Penguin Random House LLC.

Cover illustration © Mike Heath

The Library of Congress has established a Cataloging-in-Publication record for this title.

ISBN: 978-0-593-29478-9

www.penguinrandomhouse.com/large-print-format-books

FIRST LARGE PRINT EDITION

Printed in the United States of America

10 9 8 7 6 5 4 3 2 1

This Large Print edition published in accord with the standards of the N.A.V.H.

CHOPPY WATER

1

A platoon of Secret Service agents led Stone Barrington and Holly Barker from a service elevator and down a hallway, where they paused at a set of double doors.

"Ready?" Stone asked Holly.

"No," she replied firmly.

"Take a few deep breaths," he advised.

She did so, then shook her shoulders.

"Ready now?" he asked, reflecting that he wouldn't be ready, either, if he had just been elected president of the United States.

"Is it too soon for me to resign the office?" Holly asked.

"Way too soon," Stone replied. He nodded at

the agent with his hand on the doorknob, and the man pushed the door open.

The crowd in the ballroom let out a noise that Stone thought happened only at riots. Holly took hold of his arm, and he led her toward the platform at the front of the room. At the bottom of the steps, he stopped. "Okay, you're on your own now."

She nodded, let go of his arm, and climbed the stairs.

Stone took a moment to look around the room and discovered that he was the only man there wearing a tuxedo. Who had not gotten the memo—them or him?

The applause went on and on while Holly beamed at the crowd until finally she began begging with her hands for them to stop and let her speak. "First," she said, "I want to introduce the vice president–elect of the United States, Sam Meriwether, of Georgia!"

To strong applause, the former senator climbed the steps on the other side of the stage, took Holly's hand, and nodded his thanks to the audience. Then he stepped back, indicating that they should direct their attention to the president-elect.

"We've all come a long way together," she said, "and there are some people I need to thank. Please hold your applause till the end, or we'll be here all night." She thanked her father and stepmother, her campaign manager and others. Twenty names later she said, "And my friend, Stone Barrington," indicating him at the edge of the platform. A spotlight caught him.

Stone had not expected this—indeed, did not welcome it—and felt a flush of heat and a flop sweat coming on. He nodded a couple of times. Photographers' strobes flashed and iPhones were held up by people in the audience. Then, mercifully, the spotlight went elsewhere, and he was able to pat his face with a handkerchief and cool down a bit. He wondered how he could gracefully get out of the room without being noticed, then realized he was stuck there as long as Holly was.

Holly made a short, graceful speech about what it meant to her to be elected president—just short enough to make the lede for all the news shows. Then she left the stage and walked around the room alone, shaking hands and exchanging air-kisses. At a signal from her, the orchestra struck up a tune and people rose and started dancing. Holly made her way back to Stone, and they were directed out a door at the rear of the platform and into a greenroom, where staff and close friends awaited. She repeated her stroll around the ballroom. A half hour later they were led out of the room, followed by Holly's father, Ham Barker, and his wife, Ginny. The next thing they knew, they were back in suite 27A, and everybody was drinking champagne.

The TV was turned off, and a pianist and a bass player offered some light jazz background.

It was two in the morning before the last friend left, and Stone was alone with Holly.

"You look a little peaky," she said to him. "God, I forgot you're just out of the hospital. Let's get you to bed."

Stone allowed her to help him undress and rehang his arm in the sling, then they settled into bed.

"What does tomorrow hold for you?" Stone asked.

"I've told the staff I want a week off, and I don't care if they like it or not," she said. "Where can we go to be alone?"

"Do we have to stay in the country?"

"Oh, yes. Traveling abroad is going to be a very big deal for the next few years."

"Then I can offer you L.A., Maine, or Key West."

"Too many people in L.A. Too hot in Key West. That leaves Maine."

"Do you have a coat?"

"I can go shopping in the morning."

"Really? And cause a riot on Madison Avenue?"

"Oh. All right. I'll have somebody bring a few in for me to choose from." She waited for a response. "Stone?"

But Stone was out for the night.

The following morning after breakfast, Holly summoned her Secret Service head-of-detail, Bill Wright, and his deputy, Claire Dunn, and bade them to sit down. They did so.

"All right, Bill, Claire, here it is: Stone and I are going away for a week."

Their faces fell simultaneously. "Away?" Bill asked. "Where?"

"To an island in Maine," Stone said, "called Islesboro, to a village called Dark Harbor, to my house." Bill started to object, but Stone raised a hand. "Let me brief you first. The island has a winter population of about twenty this time of year. My house was built for my late cousin, Dick Stone, under the supervision of the CIA; Dick was its deputy director, and the house is bulletproof, including the windows. The nearest airport that can take a jet is Rockport, with runways of four and five thousand feet. Two ways to get to the island: ten minutes in my Cessna 182, for five people and luggage, to a 2,400-foot paved airstrip, or a twenty-minute drive to Lincolnville, where there's a ferry every hour or so. I'm not sure what the winter schedule is. I can house six of your agents in my guesthouse, and our cook will prepare their meals. There's a dock on the property should you want to send people by boat. We're next door to the local yacht club, which will be closed for the winter. You might contact them about using their clubhouse for recreation and meals."

"You didn't mention use of a helicopter into the Islesboro Airport," Bill said.

"Only if you want to attract news organizations with TV cameras."

"That's out," Holly said.

"Well," Bill said. "I'll have to contact my boss in Washington to get permission for this excursion, and I'll have to call on the Air Force for an aircraft."

"Sorry," Stone said, "I didn't mention that I own a Gulfstream 500, based at Teterboro, which will seat up to twelve people, for the leg to Rockland."

"We'll still need Air Force pilots," Bill said.

"I have a full-time pilot, highly qualified. If you want an Air Force pilot to fly right seat, fine with me."

"I'll call Washington," Bill said.

"Hold on, Bill," Holly interjected. "I want you and Washington to understand that we are not requesting permission for anything. I've made the decision to go. If your people don't want to participate, we'll be quite happy with the transportation on hand. The security arrangements are up to you."

"Yes, ma'am," Bill said.

Claire spoke up for the first time. "Mr. Barrington, I understand that you have a knife wound to your arm that requires daily inspection and rebandaging."

"That's correct."

"I'm a nurse practitioner, so I can take care of that. I'll bring the necessary materials along."

"Thank you," Stone said.

"Now," Holly said. "I propose that we leave the Carlyle at six AM tomorrow morning for Teterboro."

"I'll arrange everything," Bill said, and the two agents left.

"Now," Holly said. "I'll have to do some shopping, and I imagine that you need some proper clothing, too." She picked up the phone and called somebody.

Stone called Joan and asked her to pack a couple of bags and send them to the hotel.

7

2

They departed the Carlyle at five AM, instead of six, for better traffic conditions. They were on the ramp at Teterboro by five-thirty and attracted no attention while boarding. Faith, Stone's pilot, introduced them to her Air Force copilot; there was no stewardess on board for the short trip.

They were allowed an early takeoff and given a clearance of direct Rockland. Forty minutes later they set down. There Stone, Holly, and the head-of-detail Secret Service agents, Bill and Claire, got into Stone's Cessna, while the other agents boarded a couple of SUVs for the drive to Lincolnville and the ferry. The two pilots had accommodations in Rockland.

"The yacht club has given us the use of their building," Bill said, "and we're taking in our own bunks and a cook. We'll be out of your hair most of the time. Claire and I will use your guesthouse, if that's all right."

"Certainly," Stone said, taxiing into position.

They landed at Islesboro fifteen minutes later, and Seth Hotchkiss was there with the 1938 Ford Woodie station wagon to transport them to the house.

Once at the house, Stone showed the agents around, then they left for the yacht club to get that organized.

Stone lit a fire, and he and Holly settled down before it with cups of cocoa.

"This is all I want to do while we're here," Holly said, "just sit and stare into the fire."

"I imagine your brain will be occupied with other things," Stone said, as her cell phone rang. She switched it off. "I can return calls later." She snuggled next to him.

"What's in the big briefcase?" Stone asked.

"Three big briefcases," she said. "The rest are in the SUV, on their way. They contain lists of potential cabinet appointees and their dossiers, appointments to the Supreme Court and others, legislative proposals, executive orders to be signed on inauguration day, et cetera, et cetera. We've taken a whole motel in Rockland for staffers, and some of them will show up each day with briefing papers. There are two press pool people, sworn to secrecy and not to publish until we leave here. A press announcement is being made that I'm bound for an undisclosed location in Florida for a few days of rest and planning and will have no visitors. **Everybody** in Washington wants to visit."

"I can imagine."

They had lunch, just the two of them, and the Secret Service people were invisible, as promised. After lunch, Stone went into the village to the store to pick up a **New York Times.** "You want me to order it daily for you, Stone?" Billy, the owner, asked.

"Sure, Billy."

"What's going on over at your place?" Billy was also the head selectman and a human switchboard for local news and gossip.

"Just a few friends up from New York," Stone replied. "We're working on a new business proposal for next year."

"Dino and Viv along?"

"They've been invited, but it will be later in the week before they turn up."

That seemed to satisfy him, and Stone went home with his paper and a quart of ice cream.

———

Stone backed out of his parking space, just as another car pulled in next to it. When one of the two occupants opened a door, Stone saw a black leather bag full of camera equipment on the back seat. He stopped and, looking up, saw Billy standing on the store's front porch, greeting them. Stone caught Billy's eye and did a zipping motion over his mouth. Billy got it. He pointed this way and that, giving directions.

The two men got back into their car and drove off in the wrong direction.

Stone drove quickly back to the house, pulled into the garage, and pressed the button to close the door. One of the Secret Service men was guarding the front door. Stone said, "There are photographers on the island, looking for us, so get all your guys indoors and their car out of sight." The man spoke into his radio, then followed Stone inside. Stone looked out a window and saw the photographers driving toward them. He got a robe from the coat closet and tossed it to the Secret Service man. "Take off your coat and put this on," he said. When the man was properly costumed, Stone handed him his newspaper. "Answer the door and improvise," he said.

Stone heard car doors slamming and ducked back into the living room. A moment later there was the bang of the knocker on the front door. Stone directed the agent with a lift of his chin.

The man unfolded the newspaper, tied the robe, and opened the front door. "Yes?"

"Mr. Barrington?"

"No."

"May we speak to Mr. Barrington?"

"You'll need to go to New York for that," the agent said. "He's let me have his place for a few days."

"You mean he's not on the island?"

"Yes, but it's the island of Manhattan. Anything else I can do for you?"

"Yes, what's your name?"

"Why do you want to know?" the agent replied politely.

"For our story."

"No stories here," the agent said. "Good day. If you hurry, you can catch the next ferry. Otherwise it could be six or seven hours. It's a refueling day."

The two men ran for their car and fled the scene.

"You get an Oscar nomination for that one," Stone said to the man.

Holly was just coming downstairs. "I heard a car leave. Who was here?"

"A couple of photographers," Stone replied. "Al here told them a fairy tale, and they bit."

"Oh, good," she said.

Stone turned to the agent. "Was that true about the ferry?"

"It certainly was," Al said, "except for the refueling part. I've alerted our people on the mainland to stay out of sight until they're gone."

Stone went and sat down next to Holly. "How did they get on to us?"

"Maybe a local ashore," Al said. "Your airplane's in the hangar, isn't it?"

"Yes, and locked up."

"We can't have them looking up the tail number. If you like, I can call the FAA and have your number removed from the public-access registry."

"What a good idea," Stone said.

"Al," Holly said, "can you have his face removed, too?"

"I'll see what I can do," Al replied.

3

Stone was reading the **Times** when a cell phone rang. "It's not me," he said, to nobody in particular.

Holly produced a phone from a pocket. "It's Ham," she said. "Hey, Ham."

"Hey, baby. There was a story in the papers this morning, said you were somewhere in Florida. I had to run off a couple of people before breakfast. Are you okay?"

"Yes, I'm fine. I'm . . . Remember that place I told you about?"

"Yeah."

"I'm there."

"I'll put up a sign," he said, and told her his

idea. "Have a good time," Ham said, then hung up.

Holly hung up, too. "The Florida story in the papers worked. Ham's had visitors."

"If they knew how good a shot Ham is, they wouldn't have bothered him," Stone said.

"He's putting up a sign on the gate saying 'She ain't here, and the dog bites.'"

Stone laughed. "Do you think that will stop them?"

"No, but it'll make them think twice."

"Whose cell phone are you using?"

"A campaign worker's. She's driving home to see her folks in Texas this week, with mine in her handbag."

"That'll keep 'em busy."

"You'd better not use yours," she said.

"It's turned off. Joan can call me on the land-line, if she needs me."

As if on cue, the landline rang. "Al, will you get that? If it's a woman, it could be my secretary, Joan."

Al picked it up. "It's Joan," he said.

Stone picked up the extension on the coffee table. "Hey."

"Hey, yourself," she said. "You've had a dozen callers this morning."

"Tell them I'm on my way to Texas, driving."

"Okay. Dino says he and Viv will be at Rockland around noon today."

"I'll have the Cessna pick them up. Is he using a police aircraft?"

"Yes."

"That'll work." Dino Bacchetti was Stone's old NYPD partner who was now New York City's police commissioner. Dino's wife, Vivian, was COO of Strategic Services, the second-largest security company in the world.

"Anything else?"

"Nothing that can't wait until you're back."

"Bye." Stone hung up. "Al, New York City's police commissioner and his wife are arriving at noon at Rockland. Can one of your guys fly them over to the island in my 182?"

"I've got three who are licensed," Al said. "I'll pick one."

He got on his radio.

Stone held off lunch until the Bacchettis arrived. They got settled in, then went down to the dining room.

"Anybody bugged you up here?" Dino asked.

"We blew off a couple this morning," Stone said. "They've tried Ham's place in Florida, too."

"You know about not using cell phones?"

"Sure. Holly's using a friend's, who's driving hers to Texas this week."

"Nice move," Dino said. "Holly, did you get a lot of fan mail in the way of death threats during the campaign?"

"Not what I would call a lot," she said. "Just the usual alt-right nuts. I passed them on to the Secret Service."

"You should expect to get your share of those, Stone," he said. "You'll be surprised at how popular you're going to get."

"Holly and I are going to be in different cities most of the time," Stone said. "That'll help a little, I think."

They finished lunch and had coffee in the living room, by the fire.

"Viv," Stone said, "where are you just in from?"

"Sydney, Australia, and San Francisco, where I had a little time to catch up with my jet lag. Holly, we haven't congratulated you properly: we're so happy you won."

"Thank you, Viv. I'm still sort of in limbo—can't quite believe it. That's why I'm so happy to be up here with you all."

Bill and Claire came into the living room "Excuse us for disturbing you, ma'am," Bill said, "but Claire and I have to run over to the mainland for a security meeting. We've rented a house in Lincolnville, so we'll foot it on the ferry. All our people are either on post around the house or over at the yacht club."

"See you later, Bill," Holly said.

"Yacht club?" Viv asked. "They're sailing?"

Holly laughed. "No, they've rented the clubhouse for bunk and rec space. They can watch TV and play Ping-Pong during their off hours."

Viv stood up. "C'mon, Dino, let's get some of this unaccustomed fresh air. A walk would do us good."

Dino put aside his **Times** and got up. "I'm okay with that," he said. They got their coats on and left.

"What would you like to do this afternoon?" Stone asked Holly.

Holly walked over to the window and looked out over Penobscot Bay. Stone's dock was only yards away.

"Is that your little yacht?" she asked.

"Yes, it's called a Concordia."

"What I'd really love is a sail."

"Then why don't we have a sail?"

"If we tried, it would cause a kerfuffle with the Secret Service. They'd have to find a boat, then follow us."

"Oh."

"Stone, do you have a sail bag in the house?"

"Sure. In the garage, where the spares are."

Fifteen minutes later, Stone left the house, a big sail bag over his shoulder. The Secret Service man at the rear of the house met him. "Going somewhere, Mr. Barrington?"

"Yes, I'm going to try out a new sail on my boat."

"Where's the president-elect?"

"She's upstairs having a nap, and she doesn't want to be disturbed."

"Right, sir." He returned to his post.

Stone reached the dock and stepped into the cockpit of the yacht, then unlocked the companionway hatch and opened it. He lowered the sail bag carefully below. "Okay, the coast is clear," he said, "as long as you don't come on deck just yet."

The sail bag's zipper opened, and Holly struggled out. "I'm good."

"Just have a seat in the saloon. It'll take me a few minutes to get underway. And if you will, go up forward and hand me the genoa. The bag is labeled."

Holly found and handed the sail up to him. Stone bent it onto the forestay, then went aft and got the engine started. Shortly, they were motoring out of the harbor, past a line of mostly empty moorings.

"You can come up now," Stone said, "but sit on the cockpit floor. Those guys have binoculars, and I don't want them to spot you."

Holly tossed up some cushions, then came up the companionway steps and crawled aft, making herself a comfortable perch in the cockpit.

Stone hoisted the main and the genoa, switched off the engine, and let the boat reach along in the light winds. Soon they turned the point and were in the bay proper, the house and the yacht club now out of sight.

"What a day for it!" Holly yelled. "I feel free again. I haven't felt that way since the campaign started!"

"We're not going to see a lot of traffic out here in November, but if we spot somebody, resume your seat on the cockpit floor," Stone said.

The breeze picked up a little, and their speed increased.

4

They had been out for a good two hours when Stone felt a gust for the first time. He looked aft and saw low, dark clouds on the horizon. "Uh-oh," he said.

"You didn't get a forecast?" Holly asked. "Bad Stone!"

"I was too busy smuggling your ass onto the boat!" Stone came back. "Stand by to luff up!" He turned into the wind and the boat slowed. "Let's get these big sails down, and put up a small jib. Find me one up forward."

Holly sprang to it.

Stone cranked the main down and into the reefing boom and secured it, then freed the genoa halyard, while Holly came out the forward hatch with a jib and started pulling the genoa into the forepeak. Shortly, she had the small jib clipped onto the forestay and the halyard affixed to the sail, and Stone hauled on the halyard, which led aft to the cockpit for shorthanded sailing. He pulled in the jib sheet and winched it to the proper angle, then bore away toward home.

An hour later the sky had darkened, and big drops of scattered rain were falling on them. Stone sent Holly below for foul weather gear, and they suited up before the rain became steady.

"That's the right sail for this," Holly said.

"Yes, I think we can ride it all the way in."

The wind was increasing, and whitecaps appeared on the dark water. "Twenty knots, by the Beaufort scale," Stone said. Lightning flashed. Then they got a big gust, and the yacht heeled. "That's thirty knots," he said. The sea was choppy now, with waves of three or four feet. They pressed on, in rain and increasing fog.

"There!" Stone said, pointing at a boat. "That motor yacht is the outermost one on the mooring line." Other boats and a lot of empty moorings began appearing. They were running down a sort of alley between the rows. "We're right on course for my dock," he said. "Tell me when you spot it."

Holly went below, then her head popped up through the forward hatch. "Nothing yet!" she yelled. Then, a moment later: "Dock ho! Come five degrees to port."

Stone made the slight turn, then saw the dock. He started the engine, then dropped the jib, and Holly climbed on deck, a mooring line in her hands.

Stone eased alongside the dock and stepped ashore with the stern line and made it fast, then he went back aboard and cut the engine.

Holly stuffed the jib into the forepeak, then went below and emerged into the cockpit. It was raining hard now, and the wind was up even more.

"I don't think we'll bother smuggling you into the house," Stone said. "Nobody can see us in all this, anyway." He got the cockpit a little neater, then locked the hatch and took Holly's hand while she climbed onto the dock. He followed, and they began staggering toward the house, against the wind. Finally, its shape emerged from the gloom.

"Where's our agent on the back door?" Holly asked.

"He's taken shelter. Drowning isn't one of their duties, is it?"

"Quite right."

They shed their foul weather gear on the back porch and stuffed it into a locker to keep it from blowing away, while Stone unlocked the back door.

It was warmer inside, but the fire had died. Stone rebuilt it. Shortly, they were comforting themselves with bourbon and a blaze.

"I guess Dino and Viv got caught out, too. They must have taken shelter somewhere." A moment later, the doorbell rang, and there was hammering on the door. "That's them." Stone went to let them in.

Dino and Viv stumbled into the house, soaking wet.

"Where the hell have you been?" Dino demanded.

"Holly and I went for a sail," Stone replied.

"Lovely day for it," Dino said, backing up to the fire. "Is there such a thing as Scotch whisky in this house?"

"You two go upstairs and change," Stone said, "and we'll have drinks for you when you come back down."

The two climbed the stairs, carrying their wet shoes. Ten minutes later they were back, dry and changed. Stone handed Dino his usual Johnnie Walker Black and made Viv a martini.

CHOPPY WATER

"Where are the Secret Service people?" Dino asked, after a gulp of his Scotch.

"Bill and Claire are on the mainland, at a meeting," Stone said. "I guess the others are taking shelter at the yacht club. Nobody should have to stand outside in this rain and wind."

"Oh, yeah," Dino said, "you forgot to tell us about that."

"The vagaries of Maine weather," Stone replied. "Luckily, we had time to get our sails down and into foul weather gear before it got serious."

Holly's borrowed cell phone rang, and she answered it. "Yes? Hello, Bill. Where are you? We guessed as much. We just got back from sailing, and the Bacchettis from a walk." They could hear his raised voice. "Now, take it easy, it's not their fault. We sneaked out of the house to the dock and sailed away. All is well." She listened, then hung up.

"Bill is upset with us," she said, "and with his detail, too. He and Claire are stuck in Lincolnville for the moment; the ferry won't sail in this weather. Oh, Seth and Mary are stuck there, too; they went in for groceries."

It was getting darker, so they switched on the living room lights while Stone put more logs on the fire, then they all sat down with a second drink.

"I'm hungry," Dino said.

Holly got to her feet. "Come on, Viv. Let's see if we can find something to snack on before we get any drunker." The two of them disappeared into the kitchen. The lights went off, then came back a couple of seconds later.

"The generator has kicked in," Stone said. "At moments like this, I'm glad we have it."

"Does this bother you at all?" Dino asked.

"What? The weather?"

"No, the Secret Service. There was no one at the front door, and we sheltered out there, sort of, for half an hour, until you finally let us in."

"There was no one at the back door, either," Stone said. "With all of us gone, I guess they took refuge at the yacht club."

"Do you have a phone number for them?"

"Only for Bill, but he's stuck on the mainland."

"Call him and ask if he's in touch with his detail."

Stone dialed Bill's cell phone from the landline. "Yes?"

"Bill, it's Stone. Have you been in touch with your detail?"

"No, the cell service on the island must have gone down."

"But you reached Holly."

CHOPPY WATER

"That was before the weather got really bad. I didn't bring a handheld radio to our meeting, but as soon as we're across to the island, I'll round up everybody. I'm sure there's nothing to worry about. We hear there'll be a break in the weather soon, long enough for us to get across."

They hung up. Stone looked across the room at Dino, who had his pistol out of its holster and was shoving in a magazine and working the action.

"What's wrong?" Stone asked.

"I don't know, but something. I'm going over to the yacht club and check on those guys."

"I'll come with you," Stone said. He opened a concealed room that had been his cousin Dick's office and found himself a gun and ammo, then got them both some dry foul weather gear.

"It's letting up a little," Stone said, grabbing a pair of Surefire flashlights and tossing one to Dino. "Let's go."

They left the house by the back door.

5

Stone tucked his weapon under his slicker to keep it dry and inside his waistband to keep it handy. Dino was wearing a shoulder holster.

They stepped off the back porch into a steady, heavy rain. There was an occasional flash of lightning, followed quickly by a crash of thunder. Gusts of wind occasionally blew. They walked, sometimes waded, along the fifty-yard gravel path to the yacht club. Stone could hear an occasional thump, and as they got nearer to the entrance, he could see the right half of the French doors, banging against the side of the building. Most of its glass panes were broken.

Dino got inside first, and Stone saw his flashlight come on. "Jesus Christ!" Dino yelled. Stone switched on his own flashlight and stepped inside, waving it around, "Oh, shit," he said, as splashes of blood and gore on the walls came into view. He moved the light's beam down and began to see bodies on the floor—torn and twisted.

Dino was going from man to man and looking closer. "All of them are dead," he said, feeling an occasional wrist or throat. "And cold. A couple of hours, maybe."

"Freeze!" a man's voice shouted.

"Bill?" Stone called.

"Who's that?"

"Stone Barrington and Dino Bacchetti. Don't shoot us."

Bill Wright, followed closely by Claire Dunn, came into the room, weapons drawn. "What the hell happened?" Bill asked. "We just got here on the ferry."

"We just got here, too," Stone replied. "Dino says they're all dead, maybe for a couple of hours."

The two Secret Service agents made their own quick check. "Where is Peregrine?" Bill asked, using Holly's Secret Service code name.

"Upstairs at my house, with Viv Bacchetti."

Bill made a move in that direction.

"Hold on!" Stone said.

The agents stopped.

"They're both armed, and since they're both ex-cops, they know how to handle themselves, so identify yourself before you go inside. Wait, I'll let you in the back door." Stone led the group back to the house and opened the rear door with his key. "Holly!" he shouted. "Where are you?"

"Upstairs!" Holly called back.

"Bill and Claire are with us. Don't shoot anybody, it's safe."

"The hell it is," Bill said.

Holly and Viv came down the stairs cautiously, guns in hand. "What's wrong?" Holly asked.

"Everything," Stone replied.

Bill grabbed the landline and started dialing numbers.

"Stone," Holly said, "what's going on?"

"There's been an attack. Bill," Stone said, "you'd better make your next call to the state police. This is their jurisdiction. I've got the number." He began searching his contacts list.

"Fuck 'em," Bill said, dialing another number. "Our people are federal employees, so the FBI has jurisdiction. I'll do what I can, until they show up." He went back to his phone call. "Jerry, this is Bill Wright, Secret Service. My detail for the president-elect has been attacked: six dead, no wounded." He gave the man their location and directions, then hung up. "The FBI are getting their people down here from the state capital. Should be here in an hour."

He made another call. "I want you to get that ferry over to the island stat," he said into the phone. "If the crew has left for the day, roust 'em out and get them over here, but don't make more of a fuss than you have to. We don't want to call attention to ourselves." He hung up.

Stone checked the weather radar on his cell phone. "Uh-oh," he said. "When did anybody last look at the weather?"

"Last night," Dino said. "Are you talking about Hurricane Zelda?"

"I am."

"She's going to pass east of Newfoundland."

"Not anymore, Bill. She's taken a left, and the eye will now pass west of Nova Scotia. That's why we're getting all these bands of rain."

"We're going to be in a hole, a quiet spot, in an hour or so, and the FBI chopper can't leave until then. You've got some time to call whoever else you have to.

"The first order of business is to keep the president-elect safe," Bill said.

"Accomplished," Stone said. "There are six guns in this room, and whoever made that mess at the yacht club is gone. They must be in a boat, because the ferry has been inop. How did you get here?"

"They agreed to make a run when the wind dropped," Bill said.

"What's your plan?" Stone asked.

"We've got an unmarked helicopter at the airport, but it can't fly until the weather passes, so we're going immediately by car. You people pack your bags, and we'll get everyone in our vehicles."

Seth Hotchkiss came into the room. "Evening," he said. "What time would you like dinner?"

"I don't think we're going to have time for dinner, Seth," Stone said. "We'll be leaving shortly."

Seth nodded and left.

"Seth and his wife crossed on the ferry with us," Bill said.

"All right," Holly said. "Nobody's going anywhere until I've been told what's going on, so stop ignoring me. What mess at the yacht club?"

"Holly," Stone said. "The rest of your detail has been shot and killed at the yacht club. How many, Bill?"

"Six."

Holly stood, openmouthed. "We'd better get packed, then," she said, finally.

A half hour later, the six of them were jammed into a large, three-rowed SUV, their luggage in another behind them, all waiting for the ferry to show. The weather had passed, for the moment, and visibility was fair.

"Where are we going, Bill?" Holly said.

"To our backup location; about a forty-five-minute drive from Lincolnville. We'll do it in less than that."

"You have a backup location already?"

"We've had it since I first heard about this trip," he replied. "It was on a list we keep for possible hideouts. Don't worry, you'll be very comfortable there."

The ferry hove into view, and minutes later they were crossing. Bill wouldn't let anyone get out of the car on the crossing, and when they were ashore, the cars turned right, keeping their speed down until they were out of sight of Lincolnville.

"As soon as this hurricane passes, I'll have to go to Washington," Bill said.

"On the carpet?" Holly said.

"You guessed it."

"Bill, you haven't done anything wrong."

"I've put the president-elect of the United States in jeopardy and lost six men."

"It was a planned attack," Stone said. "You couldn't have foreseen that."

"It's my job to foresee, and I failed."

The car sped up, and Stone saw the speedometer at eighty.

"I'm more concerned with how these people found us," Stone said. "This was a spur-of-the-moment decision, and nobody could have known where we were going."

"Somebody knew," Bill said.

Everybody went quiet, and the big vehicle hurtled on through the night. They drove off the main highway and along a series of back roads, then made a right onto a larger road and crossed a short bridge. Stone looked around. "This is Mount Desert Island," he said. Bill said nothing.

They drove through the village of Somesville, so Stone knew that Somes Sound was to their left. Shortly after leaving the village they turned left, in the direction of the water, and drove very slowly along a winding road with signs proclaiming a 15 mph speed limit.

Finally, they came to a gate, and another SUV, blocking it, drove out and parked in order to allow them to drive through. They climbed a cobblestone driveway and came to a halt before a columned entrance.

"Welcome to Broad Cove Cottage," Bill said, and they all dismounted.

Right on cue, it began to rain again, and the wind was rising.

6

Stone and Holly were shown upstairs to a large master suite, with separate baths and dressing rooms. They showered and changed, then went downstairs, through a comfortable living room with many pictures, and into the kitchen, where Bill Wright sat at the kitchen table, making notes. There were two thick porterhouse steaks on the grill, sizzling, tended by an agent they hadn't seen before.

"Come in and sit down, please," Bill said. "That's Jim," pointing at the cook, "who's in charge of feeding us. Dinner's in about twenty minutes. Would you like a drink?"

Stone spotted a wet bar tucked into a corner

and, after a nod from Holly, poured them both a Knob Creek on the rocks, then sat down.

"Let me try to bring you up to date," Bill said. "First of all, I spoke to my chief. I'm not being sacked; I'll be with you for the duration."

"The duration of what?" Holly asked.

"Of the hurricane, at the very least. Also, we can't leave here until we have an operational plan to get you out of here."

"To where?" Holly asked.

"Wherever you need to go. By the way, I spoke to the president a few minutes ago, and she'd like you to call her after dinner." He gave her a slip of paper with a number on it and an iPhone. "This is your new phone. Much like the one you used at State, you can scramble when you speak to her."

Holly tucked the phone and number into a jacket pocket.

"Now," Bill said, "to address your question, Stone, about how our adversaries found us. It might not have been so hard. They could have followed us from the hotel. They could have had people at Teterboro who spotted you; same at Rockland, since you're known to have a house up here. There's no leak in our detail, because most of us are dead; Claire and I would have been, too, if we hadn't been on the mainland."

"That makes sense," Stone said. "I suggest that, as soon as weather permits, we get Faith and your pilot, who are staying on the mainland, to move my airplane to Bar Harbor Airport, which is fifteen minutes from here. I have a hangar there. If anyone sees them leave Rockland, it won't be obvious where they're going. They won't file a flight plan, and there's no tower there."

"Good idea. I'd rather fly out of here in your airplane than in a helicopter." He checked his notes: "We have a detail of twelve here, and six, including Claire and me, will travel with you. We'll be met at the other end, wherever that is, with a fresh team."

"We can seat up to twelve," Stone said. "That okay with you, Holly?"

"I expect so. Ask me sooner to the time."

"Please, ma'am," Bill said. "Please remember that—and I say this with the best intentions in the world—you're not president yet, and I won't take orders from you unless I agree with them."

"Of course, Bill. I don't mean to seem imperious."

"Plenty of time for that later," Bill said, smiling.

"Quite right."

Claire came in through the rear door of the house and greeted them all.

"Now," Bill said. "Commissioner and Mrs. Bacchetti are in the garden room, downstairs, and two agents are in the room next to theirs. Each has its own bath. Our off-duty people are in the guesthouse, and we've got two dogs, too; they're out patrolling now."

There were footsteps on the stairs and Dino and Viv came in and took seats at the table.

"We're stuck here for a while," Stone said.

Dino picked up a remote control and turned on the large TV next to the wet bar, then tuned in the Weather Channel and muted the sound. "Holy shit," he said, looking at the mass on the screen.

"Exactly," Bill said.

The cook/agent asked them to move while he set the table, and shortly, they were served the beef, roast potatoes, and green beans. Bill uncorked two bottles of wine. "We were told by the owners to help ourselves to their cellar," he said.

They had a very good dinner, without much conversation, then Holly looked at her watch and said, "I'd better make that call." She got up and took her phone into the living room next door.

———

Hello, Holly," President Katharine Lee said.

"Hello, Kate."

"I'm relieved to hear that you're all right."

"Thank you, so am I."

"You're in good hands with Bill and Claire. They've been on the White House detail for some time now. Listen to them, and don't countermand them unless you're sure you're right."

"I understand."

"You've got good company in Stone and the Bacchettis, too, so you won't be short on brains. Except for my husband and you, I value Stone's judgment more than anyone else's I can think of."

"Thank you, Kate. Are Will and Billy all right?"

"They're very well, thank you, and very concerned about your safety."

"Thank them for me."

"We're going to withhold any announcement of what happened on Islesboro, in the hope that we can make progress in the investigation early on, so you won't be seeing anything about it on TV. The weather and the small number of people on the island helped, too. Most of the winter residents left because of the hurricane, and by the time they get back, the yacht club will have been restored to its original condition."

"That's all to the good."

"There's no need to emerge from your seclusion for the time being. Go wherever you like, weather permitting."

"Thank you."

"I'll say good night, then. Continued good luck."

"Good night, Kate." Holly hung up and went back to the kitchen, where she found blueberry pie being served.

"Everything okay?" Stone asked.

"Fine," Holly replied. "They're keeping all of this from the public for as long as possible. That will make it easier for us to move around."

"I spoke to Faith and she and her copilot will move the airplane to Bar Harbor as soon as weather permits."

"Good."

From somewhere outside, they could hear the barking of a dog.

"Not to worry," Bill said, "he's not angry, just enthusiastic."

"How can you tell?"

"You get to know their voices after a while, like that of an old friend."

7

Stone woke a little before seven, as was his custom, and ran a finger down Holly's spine. She turned and came into his arms. There was no talking, just plain, hungry sex, until they were both exhausted.

"I asked for breakfast up here at seven-thirty," Holly said.

"You know me too well."

"Why is it so dark at this hour?"

Stone got up, found the cord, and swept open twelve feet of curtains. It didn't get much brighter in the room. Rain was still falling, sometimes traveling horizontally, and the large trees outside were bending with the wind. At the bottom of the large rear garden, which swept down to Broad Cove, he could see a dock, where a Hinckley motor yacht was moored, at times obscured by rain. The cove was sheltered enough that the wind did not disturb it unduly, just created whitecaps.

"Wow!" Holly said, sitting up on the side of the bed. "So that's what a Maine hurricane looks like."

Stone turned on the TV and found the Weather Channel. "It's not the whole thing, just the western edge."

There was a knock at the door and a male voice shouted, "Breakfast!"

"Just a moment, please!" Holly shouted back. They both found robes in their respective dressing rooms, then she went to the door and let Jim, carrying a large tray, into the room. "Just set it on the bed, Jim," she said, and he did, then left.

"Seven-thirty sharp," Stone said.

They got back into bed and used their remote controls to raise them into sitting positions. Stone found a morning program and they listened to the news, while they tucked into their sausages and eggs.

Toward the end of the half hour, a good photograph of Holly appeared on-screen, and the young news reader said, "President-elect Holly

Barker continues her disappearing act, having not been spotted anywhere on the Eastern Seaboard, or elsewhere for that matter. You go, girl!"

Holly got a laugh out of that.

"What do you want to do today?" Stone said.

"Oh, I don't know, how about a long walk?"

Stone laughed. "Check in with me when you get back."

"You mean you don't want to be soaking wet and windburned?"

"I mean exactly that."

"Well, there's plenty to read," she said, indicating the bookcase surrounding the TV.

"And there are more on the shelves on the landing, outside our door, and there's a study somewhere downstairs."

The lights and TV suddenly went out, but five seconds later they came back on.

"There's a generator, just like at my house."

The satellite TV took a minute or two to reset before the picture was restored.

There was another knock on the door.

"Come in!" Holly shouted.

Dino and Viv walked in. "Tennis, anyone?" Dino said.

"Water polo, more likely," Stone replied.

"Viv has put a gun to my head and demanded

a walk. So we're going to take some boots and slickers from the mudroom two floors down and wander down the road, see who we see."

"Better you than me," Stone said.

"I'll come," Holly said. "Give me five minutes." She headed for her dressing room with Viv tagging along.

Dino turned around one of the two armchairs facing the TV and sat down. "Well, it's not exactly what we'd planned, is it?"

"None of it," Stone said. "I think Holly's still depressed about what happened to her detail. Thanks for suggesting the walk. I think trying not to drown will put her mind at ease for a while."

"It is goddamned awful out there. Maybe I'll let the two go by themselves."

"There'll be at least four agents along," Stone said, "and maybe a dog. The summer people have gone, but maybe there's a year-round resident or two. Tell her not to get recognized."

"I think they should send an agent ahead to warn them if somebody pops up. Then they can turn back," Dino said.

The women came back. "Ready, Dino?"

"I'm chickening out," Dino said. "Send up a pot of coffee, will you? Maybe Stone and I can find an old movie on TV."

As he said that, the picture on the TV seemed to shatter into pieces.

"Satellite TV doesn't like heavy precip," Stone said. "You'd better find a book." He pointed at a long line of small books on the top shelf over the TV. "There's the complete works of P. G. Wodehouse; that should keep you in laughs for a few weeks."

"Suit yourself," Holly said. "Oh, there's something I want to show you, Stone, if you can get out of bed long enough."

Stone struggled to his feet. "Lead on."

She led him out of the room to the landing, where there was a pair of wing chairs and a bookcase covered a wall. "All World War II history and biography," Holly said.

"Wonderful!" Stone enthused.

"But that's not what I wanted to show you." She took hold of the center of the bookcase and pulled. The case swung open, revealing a kitchenette and laundry room behind it.

"Ah, a good place for Dino and me to hide, if the bad guys show up." She closed it again, making it a seamless bookcase again.

"We're off," Holly said, and she and Viv went downstairs. Stone and Dino went back into the bedroom, turned the chairs toward the TV, and pulled up their ottomans. Jim came in with a pot of coffee and cups and set it all on the table between them, then went back downstairs.

Dino poured them a cup each. "I've been talking with Bill Wright about who the assailants were on Islesboro."

"Any conclusions?"

"He got a call from the FBI while we were talking. The Bureau thinks we're dealing with some sort of militia—white supremacists, probably."

"I suppose it could be."

"They could be misogynists, as well," Dino said. "The reasoning is that while having a woman as president was bad, having two in a row is intolerable. At least one group has been suggested by a watchdog group in Alabama, but nobody has taken credit."

"Well, thank God for that," Stone said. "If somebody takes credit, the media will know it happened and go nuts. That would make it a lot more difficult for us to move around, assuming we want to."

"I think we should stay here for as long as everybody can stand it," Dino said.

"Okay with me," Stone said, "but eventually, cabin fever will set in, and we'll have to find a new cabin."

8

Two agents and a German shepherd awaited on the front porch, and the group, wearing rubber boots and swathed in waterproof clothing that concealed the agents' guns, started down the driveway. They could now see that the property was surrounded by deer fencing, and they let themselves out through a pedestrian gate next to the main gate, which was blocked by a black SUV, resting on the deer grate that barred the animals from entry.

Holly and Viv started down the road, which was somewhat sheltered by forest on either side. Holly looked to her left and saw an agent wading. Apparently, there was a swamp on that side of the road. They passed a couple of houses that appear unoccupied and continued down the road. They had climbed a little hill and reached the top, when Viv spotted the blood.

"Everybody stop," she said, holding up both hands.

"What is it, Mrs. Bacchetti?" an agent asked.

"Blood on two trees, there and there," she said, pointing. There was probably a lot more of it, but the rain must have washed some away. A dog began to bark somewhere in the woods.

The agent spoke into his fist, and there was a return radio call, then a shout. "Down here!" he called.

"Ladies, please remain where you are," the detail leader said, producing a small machine gun and racking the slide. He went on talking to his fist.

An agent appeared out of the gloom from the direction of the shout, carrying something in one hand.

"What on earth is that?" Holly asked.

"It's the head of a young buck deer," the agent replied. "Appears to be a four-pointer." He raised a hand to his other agent. "Just leave it there. We don't need to see any more."

The agent tossed it back into the woods, out of

sight, then joined them on the road. "Somebody shot the deer and butchered it back about forty yards that way. Looks like somebody needed meat."

"How much of it did they take?"

"Only the haunches," the man replied.

"Could you tell what it was shot by?"

"The neck was torn up, so I reckon a military round, from an assault weapon. A hunting rifle round would have been a lot neater."

"Did you hear anything?"

"Nope, but the carcass wasn't frozen, and it was pretty cold last night, so they must have taken it early this morning. The rain and wind were noisy, so we might not have heard a single shot."

"Did they leave any tracks?"

"I saw half a footprint. It's a Vibram sole, so it could have been a hiking boot, but it's too wet back there for tracking. The dog couldn't make anything of it."

"Direction?"

"Away from the road."

"There's another road out there, called Broad Cove Road." The detail leader began talking into his fist again. Finally, he addressed Holly and Viv. "I'm sorry, ladies, but we're going to have to return to the house. Shortly, there'll be a lot of people searching these woods, and we don't want somebody to mistake us for the deer hunters." He beckoned, then they started back toward the house.

Dino and Stone were half asleep in their chairs, books in their laps, when Holly and Viv walked into the bedroom, stripped of their waterproof clothing and boots.

"That was a short walk," Stone said.

Holly explained their experience.

"Well, they didn't come this way," Dino said, "or they'd have run into an agent or two, maybe even you."

"So," Viv said, "what do we do now?"

"Find a book," Dino said.

"We'll go down to the study," Holly said, "and leave you two alone." They went back downstairs.

The study was at the opposite end of the house from the kitchen and contained a corner computer station, a sofa, a pair of wing chairs, and a large fireplace. There was a turret at the other end of the room, with a circular staircase, and under that a coffee table and an Eames lounge chair next to the windows.

Holly went to a bookcase, and her eye immediately fell on a title: **1942, The Year That Tried Men's Souls,** by Winston Groom. She took it and settled into the Eames chair.

Immediately, a head leaned out from the turret on the upper floor. "Ma'am," he said, "I'm afraid that's an insecure location. You're too easily seen from outside."

"Right," Holly said, and moved further inside to a wing chair and turned on a floor lamp next to it.

Viv was already settled on the sofa. "Would you like a fire?" she asked.

"Oh yes."

The fireplace was already laid with hardwood. Viv found a gas valve and a box of long matches, and immediately had a blaze going.

"Much better," Holly said.

Later, Bill Wright knocked on the doorjamb and came into the room. "Lunch in half an hour," he said.

"Any result from your search party?" Holly asked.

"They found some truck tracks on a neighboring road to the south where they could have loaded their kill and driven away," he said. "No telling where they went from there."

"Thanks, Bill. Stone and Dino are upstairs. You might let them know when it's lunchtime."

Bill went away, and Holly and Viv settled back with their books.

9

Colonel Wade Sykes, U.S. Army (Ret.), sat at his desk in a book-lined, walnut-paneled study of a comfortable stone house near McLean, Virginia, working on an op-ed piece for the **Washington Stalwart,** which came close to being a paper version of Fox News, except that there was no unslanted news reporting printed in this newspaper. He wrote for them and other publications under the pseudonym Watchman. The cell phone in his shirt pocket hummed.

"Yes?"

"Are you encrypted?"

"Always, on this line."

"Would you care for some fresh venison?"

"Good God, don't tell me you've been hunting!"

"Quite by accident. We were walking the area, looking for the house, when a buck popped up, and Harold got him from the hip. Pure instinct."

"I hope it didn't wake anybody up."

"Nobody to hear it, and at that hour the wind was howling."

"Are there no people out there?"

"Apparently, it's nearly all snowbirds," Rudy said. "Last night there were lights in only one house, some distance away. We saw a car drive away very early, as if it had a long commute."

"You're sure they're not on that road?"

"We drove all the way to the point and found nothing but three or four houses, boarded up for the winter. It's a dead end, so we couldn't have missed anybody coming or going."

"As long as you're certain they're not there."

"I am."

"There's been nothing on TV or in the papers— not even the Maine papers—about the incident on Islesboro."

"Then they must be keeping it quiet."

"I expect so."

"You know, our next stop could be to go right back to Islesboro. Last place they'd look for us."

"They've got a caretaker and his wife listed for

the property, and you didn't shoot them. Also, there's the busybody storekeeper who runs the jungle telegraph on the island. There's also a guy named Rawls, ex-Agency, who practically shoots at anybody he sees. Did you check the local airports?"

"Both Rockland and Bar Harbor are dead quiet; not worth stationing a man at either of them."

"Then you might as well make a move."

"All right. What are your orders?"

"Come back to base, and we'll regroup."

"Right. Shall I bring the venison?"

"Why not?"

"We'll be there by nightfall." Rudy hung up, and Sykes went back to his piece, which put a little meat on the bones of a conspiracy theory he'd dreamed up.

By mid-morning the skies had cleared on Mount Desert Island, and Stone got a call from Faith.

"Hi, there. Where are you?"

"We just landed at Bar Harbor, and the airplane is being towed to the hangar now."

"Make yourself at home in the apartment in the hangar," Stone said. "I'll let you know when we have a plan."

"Right."

"You know where to find groceries?"

"Yep."

"Then don't starve." Stone hung up and turned to Bill Wright. They were in a little sitting room off the kitchen. "Zelda has moved offshore, and the airplane is now at Bar Harbor, ready to do our bidding."

Holly came in with a cup of tea and sat down. "This is a lovely spot, but at this time of the year, depression creeps in."

"Would you prefer a sunnier, warmer spot?"

"Yes, please. What's on offer?"

"Well, there's L.A."

"Too many reporters," Bill said.

"I have a house at the Arrington Hotel, which is quite secluded."

"You've got a house on Key West, too," Holly said.

"Fewer people to deal with," Bill said, "and we've got the naval air base, so getting in and out unnoticed wouldn't be a problem."

"Holly," Stone said. "How much longer are you planning to remain invisible?"

"Well, I guess it can't go on forever," she said. "Where's your nice, big yacht?"

"In a shed built to hold it, about fifty miles from here."

"Oh, well."

"So it's Key West, then?" Bill asked.

Holly nodded.

"How long a flight?"

"Four hours, give or take," Stone said.

"I'll buy into that, if we can take off, say, an hour after dark," Bill said.

"Done," Stone replied. "I'll alert the housekeeper and the cook."

"I'll need their names, dates of birth, and Social Security numbers—and those of anyone else who is likely to come into the house."

"There's a caretaker, too. I'll get you all that."

"Then what time shall we leave the house?"

"As soon as it's dark. There's a big moon tonight, so we might be able to get back to the main road without headlights," Stone said.

"I like the sound of that."

"In fact, when the moon's up, we might be able to taxi and take off without lights. The GPS will keep us on the center lines from hangar to takeoff."

"You're thinking the way I think, Stone. All okay with you, ma'am?"

"With you two around I don't have to think at all," she said.

Stone consulted the map Bill had given him. "Bill, exactly where are we on this map?"

Bill started a finger at Somesville and ran it along their route, then tapped on a spot.

"This is Broad Cove Cottage, right?"

"Right."

"But it's not on Broad Cove Road?"

"Nope. The name is a reference to the cove. Broad Cove Road is half a mile farther south."

"And where was the butchered deer found?"

"Right about here," Bill said, pointing to a spot. "Wait, I think I see your point. It was found about here, close to Broad Cove Road."

"Right. Perhaps these people were given the name of the house and assumed that Broad Cove Cottage was on Broad Cove Road?"

"It's a good thing they're not geniuses," Holly said.

As the moon rose, Stone entered the gate code at the Bar Harbor Airport, and the three-car motorcade drove through. The hangar doors were open, and the tow was pulling the Gulfstream onto the ramp. When the tow had departed they got out of the SUVs and the agents began loading luggage, while the passengers, plus Bill and Claire, boarded and made themselves comfortable.

Stone went forward to the cockpit. "Is it bright

enough to taxi and take off without lights?" he asked Faith, who was in the left seat, running checklists.

She looked out the windows. "Sure," she said.

"Don't file ahead of time," he said. "Do it after takeoff, with Boston Center, instead of Bangor Approach."

"I guess they won't arrest me for that," she said.

"I'll see that they don't," Bill said. "We're plugged into those guys."

"Just grand," Stone said. "When you're ready."

10

Stone stood behind the cockpit seats; he knew the airport better than Faith. "Cross the FBO ramp, then turn left, then right. That will put us parallel to runway 4/22. The windsock favors twenty-two."

"Got it," she said, taxiing along beside the runway, until the taxiway came to an end with a left turn to the runway entrance.

"Announce your presence and intention," Stone said, "but don't use our tail number."

Faith ran her pre-takeoff checklist, looked right and left to be sure there were no approaching aircraft, then pressed the push-to-talk button. "Aircraft entering runway 22 for takeoff. Anybody in the pattern?" She released the button and listened. No answer.

"Aircraft taking off on twenty-two," she said, then taxied onto the runway, checked her flap settings, put on the brakes, and pushed the throttle slowly forward, holding the aircraft in place. When the gauges showed full power, she released the brakes and began her takeoff run. She watched the screen before her, which displayed a synthetic image of the runway; it showed her on the center line. Ahead and to her left, a nearly full moon was rising, illuminating the landscape remarkably well.

"Rotate," the copilot said, and Faith pulled back on the sidestick. The aircraft left the ground and began to climb rapidly.

"Okay," Stone said, "you can light up now."

The copilot flipped switches and the exterior and interior lights came on. Faith turned on the autopilot.

"Call Boston Center at ten thousand feet, then we're on our way." Stone walked back and joined the others. The president-elect of the United States was serving drinks, and his was on the table before him. "You do good work," he said to Holly. "We may keep you on here."

The airplane made a turn to the right, and Stone looked forward at Faith. She gave him a thumbs-up.

"We're on course for Naval Air Station Key West," Stone said.

"Expect a warm reception," Bill Wright said. "We've had a word with them, and they'll have vehicles waiting to take you to your destination. Faith has probably already been cleared direct to Key West."

"Nothing like having the way paved for you," Stone said, taking his seat and picking up his drink.

"Stone," Holly said, "do you really believe these people missed us because they took the wrong road?"

"Makes sense," Stone replied. "If they'd taken the right road, they would have found a suspicious black SUV blocking the driveway at the dead end, and that would have been a tipoff, wouldn't it?"

"I suppose it would," she said. "I'm looking forward to being in your Key West house again."

"It's not bulletproof, but the place was built on the outside of the lot, around two courtyards, so there are no views of the streets or the neighbors, nor any for them of us."

Bill Wright held up an iPad with an aerial image on it. "Is this the place?"

Stone studied the image. "That's it. Google Earth?"

"Right."

"Well, at least it's a still image. Nobody can watch us having a drink around the pool. It's also a few years old. I bought new pool furniture recently, and the old furniture is in this satshot."

"Good to know."

"By the way, Bill, I don't know what your plans are for housing for your people, but one of my cars is in my hangar at Key West Airport, so you could put cots in the empty garage. Its rear entrance is off the laundry room, and there's a full bath in there that they can use."

"I'll take a look. One team will be housed on the naval base, anyway. They're already there."

Holly and Viv warmed up roast chicken in the galley's oven, then served it with rice and vegetables, while Stone retrieved a couple of bottles of good California cabernet from the wine cooler and poured them. The airplane leveled off at their assigned altitude and cruised on south through the darkness.

Looking out one of the big windows, they could see towns and villages lit up, and eventually cities, as they sped down the Eastern Seaboard at 490 knots. They picked up an offshore airway, after crossing Long Island, and got a look at the coastal cities from well out at sea.

Three hours and a half after takeoff, they set down on runway 9 at Naval Air Station Key West, on Boca Chica Field. Stone noticed a fire truck and other emergency vehicles parked near the end of the runway.

"Is that equipment for us?" Stone asked Bill.

"We're carrying precious cargo," Bill replied. "They'll follow us to our parking spot. When we're off the airplane they'll put it in one of the big hangars to prevent viewing by those who entertain themselves with satellite images, whoever they may be."

In little more than twenty minutes they were inside Stone's house, while the van carrying their luggage disgorged its contents.

"Bill," Stone said, "we're going to put you or Claire and whoever else you want, in the upstairs guest bedroom. It's the biggest."

"Don't worry, we'll manage. We've got cots in the van, if we need them."

"You'll have to park the van around the corner

after it's unloaded. The street is too narrow to accommodate it, and so is my garage."

"We've already found a ladder in your garage, and we're stationing a sharpshooter on the roof."

"Good idea," Stone said. He checked on Dino and Viv, then went to the little freestanding cottage that housed the master suite. Holly was already in bed, half asleep.

"Want some company?" Stone asked, tossing his clothes into the hamper.

"Sure, as long as he doesn't expect any action tonight. I'm bushed."

And so, he found, was he. They were soon sound asleep.

11

Colonel Wade Sykes got an encrypted phone call while having breakfast. "Yes?"

"It's me. We lost them during the night."

"How did you manage that?"

"Well, this is kind of embarrassing, but we found out this morning that Broad Cove Cottage isn't on Broad Cove Road. It's on the next road to the north. We found the other road, with a house at the end. They were gone, but left lots of car tracks in the mud. We checked the airport at Rockland, and the big hangar's door was open; nothing inside. They probably left in the middle of the night or, at least, before sunrise."

"Hang on," Sykes said, and turned to his laptop.

"This Barrington fellow has a lot of houses: one in L.A., one in Key West, two in England, and another in Paris. His airplane has the range for any of them from either Bangor or Presque Isle, one of which is where they'd have to clear customs on departure."

"Have you checked any destination airports?"

"Yes, we've checked Key West and both Burbank and Van Nuys, which are the most likely general aviation airports for an aircraft of that size. Nothing."

"Where does he land in England?"

"One of his houses is in London, the other is in the country, in Hampshire. He can land at London City, but hangarage is jammed there. He could also land at Northolt, west of the city, but the hangarage there is packed, too."

"Check Southampton and Bournemouth, in the south."

"I'll get back to you." He hung up.

Sykes was washing his dishes when the phone rang again. "Yes?"

"Bournemouth and Southampton come up zero."

"Maybe he drove someplace from Maine," Sykes suggested.

"Why would he do that? The weather has cleared, and he could go anywhere in the

Gulfstream, and much faster. We'd be wasting our time to do a search for a car, when we don't even know if or what he's driving."

"All right, shut it down and come home. Thanks for putting in the extra time on this."

"No problem. We'll be there tonight."

They both hung up.

Stone and Holly were having breakfast in bed when Stone checked his e-mail and found one from Sam Meriwether, the former senator from Georgia and the vice president–elect.

Stone,

I can't find our friend anywhere. Has she fallen off the map? If you're in touch, ask her to call me without delay; there are things afoot that she needs to know about.

Stone handed Holly the phone. "Maybe you'd better call him."

They finished breakfast, then Holly called Sam on Stone's phone.

"Well, you're alive," Sam said. "When are you planning to appear on Earth again?"

"Well, I know where I'll be on January 20."

"We need you sooner than that."

"For what?"

"We didn't have time to talk before you vanished into thin air, so nobody's had a chance to tell you that you're booked on the Sunday shows of all four networks this weekend."

"Blow them off."

"We can't do that, Holly. You've already been gone too long. You need to take a victory lap, to let the folks who voted for you see your smiling face."

"Hang on, Sam." She covered the phone. "Stone, they've got me booked on all networks Sunday morning. When would we have to leave to make them?"

"Saturday night, latest," Stone said.

"Sam says I have to do this."

"I'm all for it," Stone said. "Aren't you getting tired of hiding?"

She went back to the phone. "All right, Sam. What time do you want me, and where?"

"Seven AM, Sunday, at your house. I'm assuming the Secret Service will transport you, but I'd like to have somebody in the car with you who knows the ropes with the networks."

"Okay, have 'em ring the doorbell. The Service

will want to board me in the garage. E-mail me a schedule on this phone, and I'll pass it on to them, so they can make their arrangements. See you on the tube." She made a kissing noise, then hung up.

"Well, so much for your vacation. I'm afraid it wasn't much of one."

"At least I got in some sleep and a few drinks," she said. "Not to mention your body, and I want some more of that right now."

Stone set the breakfast trays outside the door, then dove into her waiting arms.

After taking care of that, Stone sought out Bill Wright. "We're going to need to fly to Washington tomorrow night," he said.

"What's the occasion?"

"She's booked on four television shows on Sunday, in the Washington studios of all four networks."

"May I make a suggestion?" Bill asked.

"Sure."

"Why don't we do a TV setup at her house, and she can do all four from there, remotely. She'll still be on live TV, and we won't have to secure four studios."

"I think that's a great idea," Stone said. "I'll call Sam."

"You can blame us, if you like. Tell him we're insisting for reasons of her personal security."

"Right." Stone got on the phone with Sam Meriwether and gave him the suggestion.

"I don't see why not," Sam replied. "It will give the appearance of a homier feeling. Is it too early for a Christmas tree?"

"I think so," Stone replied.

"I'll call you back."

Stone went back to the bedroom and told Holly what was up.

"Wonderful!" she enthused. "I won't have to sit around those studios waiting and being nice to people."

"Right. Sam is setting it up, and we'll offer the feed to the four stations. They won't have to do a thing but press a button. They'll love it."

Inside of an hour, everyone was in agreement.

"I guess you'll want to land at Dulles," Bill said.

"No, at Manassas, Virginia. There's enough runway, and a lot fewer people around."

"Okay, that suits us fine. Where will she want to go after that?"

"Hang on," Stone said. He went back to the bedroom. "Where do you want to go after Sunday?" he asked.

72

She seemed nonplussed.

"Your choices are: one, a prisoner in your own home; two, a prisoner in my home; three, live your life and the hell with them."

"I won't feel safe with option three," she said. "Where do you want me?"

"In New York, with me," he said firmly.

"Okay, we'll stay in New York Sunday night."

"Great!" He went to inform Bill and the Bacchettis.

12

The Gulfstream set down just after dark and a new detail of agents took over, moving passengers and luggage into SUVs and leaving the airfield in five minutes.

"Let me borrow your phone," Holly said to Stone. He handed it over, and she called the chef at her favorite local restaurant. "Hello, Danny? It's Holly Barker." There was a moment of ado before Holly could continue. "I'm on my way in from out of town with some friends who are staying at my house. Could you make them some dinner, and deliver it? There are six, and I'll leave it to you to choose the menu. Don't bother with wines. Thank you, Danny. Just put it on my tab and add a big tip." She hung up. "We will be fed in an hour," she said. "Bill, you and Claire join us. Your detail can fend for themselves."

"That'll work," Bill said.

"I suppose they'll have to sweep the house?"

"Already done," he replied. "It's clean."

They drove to Georgetown. A few yards from the house, the garage door opened and they entered the basement. A group of cots were set up in a corner, ready for use.

They dismounted and went to their rooms to freshen up. Holly stayed upstairs until the food had been delivered, then she joined everyone else. While they were in the dining room a crew arrived and began to set up camera and audio equipment. Holly went into the living room and approved the corner of the room that would be on camera, then checked out the camera angles. She rejoined the others in the dining room. "We could shoot it tonight, if they didn't all want to be live."

After dinner, the White House was on the line for Holly, and shortly, so was Kate Lee. "I understand you're safely at home and will be broadcasting from there tomorrow morning," she said to Holly.

"That is correct."

"I wonder if that might be a good time to say something about the events on Islesboro?"

"A good time for you, or for me?"

"I think it would be a good opportunity to look cool under fire. After the last interview you could be hooked up to all four stations and say a few words. I'll leave it to you what to say."

"All right, Kate, I can do that."

"Did you enjoy Key West?"

"I wasn't there long enough," Holly said, "but I enjoyed Stone. I'm going back to New York with him tomorrow and stay there for a while, gradually emerging from my shell."

"Who was it who said, 'Never miss an opportunity to have a good meal or sex'?"

"I don't know. It sounds like Oscar Wilde, though."

"Will and I are going to be in New York next Wednesday. Perhaps we could have dinner with you, Stone, and the Bacchettis."

"I'm sure Stone will enjoy hosting that, and we won't have to bother with a restaurant."

"Fine. We'll be there for drinks at six-thirty. Sleep well." She hung up.

Holly returned to the table. "Stone, Kate Lee has asked if you will give them dinner on Wednesday evening; the Bacchettis are invited, too."

"Of course I will. I'll let Helene know."

"Now, Bill. You and Claire can do your thing at Stone's house."

"Of course," he replied.

After making love with Stone, Holly went to her study, got pen and paper and wrote a couple of drafts of what she wanted to say the following day. Then she took the list of names of the murdered agents and wrote a letter to each of their next of kin, put them in envelopes, then stamped and sealed them for mailing by the Secret Service the following day.

Finally, she crept into bed beside the sleeping Stone and went to sleep.

Holly awoke at five AM and went down to the kitchen, where she had coffee, then turned herself over to the hairdresser and makeup artist. The TV director came into the room. "Good morning, ma'am," he said. "We'd like to propose a slight change in our plans this morning."

"As long as it doesn't require a costume change and new makeup," Holly said.

"Senator Meriwether thinks you might be interviewed on all four programs at once. Each would be cued when it's their turn. Then, when that's done, you can say that you have an announcement to make, and we'll cut their mics, so you won't have to deal with their reactions."

"I think that's a brilliant idea," Holly said.

"It's a one-hour show, so each of them will have about fifteen minutes, and I'll decide when to cue them. We've set up a monitor with a quartered screen, so you can look them all in the eye. Or at least, that's how it will seem to the viewers."

"Excellent."

At ten minutes before the start time, Holly was led into the living room and seated in a comfortable chair with an extra pillow for a better altitude for the camera. She was fitted with an earpiece in each ear, so that the director could speak to her without the world hearing it. "I'm in your left ear, and the questioners are in your right. Got it?"

"Got it. Oh, if it's all right, I'd like for Fox News to ask the first question. My history with them has always been a little contentious, so we might as well get that out of the way."

"I can do that," the director said. "Here we

go, in five, four, three, two, one . . ." Music and an announcer's voice came on to introduce the show. The director would moderate from off-camera.

"Good morning," he said. "And welcome to the home of our president-elect, Holly Barker. I will call on each participant for questions, which should not be longer than fifteen seconds, and the president-elect will have approximately ninety seconds to answer. Our first question comes from Fox News."

Holly looked at the woman occupying one corner of the screen before her.

"Good morning, Ms. Barker," the woman said. "I think Americans would like to know why you have been in hiding for the past week or so."

Holly smiled. "Not in hiding, but in the company of old friends in a quiet place. It gave me a little time to collect my thoughts and rest my body, after a hectic campaign schedule. I'll have more to say about that at the end of the program."

The next questions were asked, and Holly gave them thoughtful, sometimes witty, replies, exhibiting her knowledge of policy and her vivid intelligence. An hour later, they were at the end.

The director spoke up. "The president-elect has asked for a moment to say a few words on another subject," he said.

"Thank you," Holly replied. "During my time off, with friends in a secluded place that will remain unnamed, an attempt was made on my life. I was away from the house at the time, and as you can see, the attempt was not successful. However, in my absence, a tragedy occurred: six members of my Secret Service detail were attacked and killed by automatic weapons fire in a building near my quarters. The weapons were apparently silenced, because my friends and I heard nothing. I and my companions were removed to a safe location very quickly, and the Secret Service felt strongly that this announcement should be postponed until the situation was stable and pursuit of the perpetrators had begun. I could not disagree. Those violent people have not yet been brought to justice, but every available resource of law enforcement has been deployed, and I hope they will be arrested soon.

"These fallen agents gave their all to protect me, and I shall always be grateful to them. I mourn with their families, whose losses are incalculable and unbearable.

"Thank you for listening so that I could share this news with the nation. Goodbye for now."

"And out," the director said. His crew removed her earpieces and began restoring the living room to its previous order.

"Good job," Stone said, kissing her on the forehead.

13

That evening they arrived at Teterboro. The Bacchettis' car awaited them, as did Stone's. He explained the armor contained in his car.

"Who did the work?" Bill Wright asked.

"Strategic Services. They have a branch that does special vehicles."

"Have you ever put its defenses to use?"

"I had a window fired on once," Stone replied. "It stopped the bullet and starred, but it didn't shatter."

"Those people do good work," Bill said, taking the shotgun seat.

A half hour later, they were driving into Stone's

garage. "There's room for some of your vehicles," Stone said. "I own the house next door, too."

"That's convenient for us," Bill said. "Nothing says 'the Secret Service is here' like a few black SUVs parked outside."

Stone and Holly went straight up to the master suite and unpacked in their separate dressing rooms.

"It's like coming home all over again," Holly said, snuggling up close to Stone.

The following morning, Stone's cell phone rang as they were finishing breakfast.

"Good morning, Lance," he said. "I'm scrambled." Lance Cabot was the director of central intelligence, for whom Stone was an advisor.

"Good morning, Stone. How was your vacation with Holly?"

"I'm sure you've heard all the details," Stone said.

"What I haven't heard or understood is why there was no attack at your backup location?"

"We believe that they had been told to go to Broad Cove Cottage but were not told the house was not on Broad Cove Road, an understandable mistake. So they didn't get closer than about half a mile."

"Ah, fortune smiled."

"Just when we needed a smile most."

"So now Holly faces assassination attempts right up to her inauguration?"

"Possibly not. The Secret Service is operating now at post-inaugural staffing levels, and the assailants may be put off by the headlines."

"Have you seen this morning's papers?"

"Not yet. They're at the foot of the bed." Stone picked up the **Times** and shook it from its blue plastic bag. The banner headline read:

ASSASSINATION ATTEMPT ON PRESIDENT-ELECT

A still photograph of Holly during her television appearance decorated the front page.

"Got it."

"They had to tear up the front page to get that in this morning's paper," Lance said. "Usually they can't manage more than the college football scores the next day."

"It's a more important story than the football scores," Stone replied.

"Quite right. All of my people based domestically have an ear to the ground," Lance said. "I hope that will turn up something useful."

"I hope so, too," Stone said.

"Give my best to Holly," Lance said, then hung up.

"That was Lance," Stone said. "He sends his best."

"How sweet. Is he doing anything about this?" She was reading the front page.

"He says all of his people in the country have an ear to the ground."

"That must be uncomfortable for them."

"I expect so, because they will know that he means it."

"Oh?"

"Lance would like nothing better than to one-up the Secret Service and the FBI."

"He would probably expect the Medal of Freedom for it."

"Lance always has high expectations. You should know that better than anybody." Holly had once worked for Lance and had been promoted to Kate Lee's deputy, when she had been director at the CIA, crowding Lance, who would have liked the job himself.

"I'm sure he will give me plenty of opportunities to make it up to him."

"You shouldn't be too hard on Lance, Holly. He's inordinately proud of you."

"Taught me everything I know, huh?"

"Well, probably not everything."

"You go right on thinking that," Holly said.

"I'll think it. What does your day hold?"

"I have a lot of pent-up shopping urges I have to satisfy. Claire is working up a schedule and making appointments for me, so her people can stay one step ahead. We're going to use both an SUV and your car, if that's all right, just to keep photographers off my tail. One of Bill's people will drive, so we won't need Fred."

"That's fine. I have some work and correspondence to catch up on."

She kicked off the covers. "Oh, and I'm getting my hair done, too."

"Don't you have something called a transition to deal with?"

"That starts tomorrow. Sam Meriwether is assembling lists of names for court appointments and cabinet posts, as well as for the Supreme Court. I know everybody in Kate's administration pretty well, and it will help if we can persuade some of them to stay on, instead of writing their books or getting lobbying jobs."

"Good luck with that," Stone said. "The ones who were making money before serving will need to make money again."

"You could be right, but don't worry, we're covering all the bases. What job would you like?"

Stone laughed. "The one I've got now," he replied.

"You mean satisfying the chief executive's cravings on a regular basis?"

"As regularly as you can get to New York."

"They've taken a permanent suite for me at the Carlyle, and I get to decorate it, so we can alternate trysting places."

"Where's the transition team working?"

"In an empty storefront on Madison Avenue down from the Carlyle."

"All very convenient," he said.

"Especially you," she replied, kissing him. "Now I've got to get into the shower." She ran for it.

14

Holly wore a silk scarf and dark glasses as she entered Bloomingdale's. The Secret Service people worked hard at not being noticed, and Claire was her body agent for the day, since two women navigating the store didn't attract a lot of attention.

She bought much of a new wardrobe that, after tailoring, would be shipped to Stone's house, where she would use a spare bedroom as a dressing area during the transition.

Lunch was at Ralph Lauren's office on Madison, where she, the designer, and his team began talking about a special-occasion wardrobe, beginning with the inauguration and the inaugural ball. Another team would work on everyday clothes and outfits for travel to foreign countries. Stone was making a big contribution to the wardrobe, through the inaugural committee, taking care not to violate any campaign contribution laws.

She also met with an interior design group to talk about the Carlyle suite and the family quarters at the White House, plus the Oval Office. They looked at sketches for fabrics and wallpapers and rugs for the family quarters. A small army of decorators would move into the Big O the night before the swearing-in ceremony, and it would be ready for photographing and use at noon on January 20. Holly would stay at her Georgetown house for as long as it took them to do up her quarters.

When she got back to Washington she would be given a tour of the National Gallery and allowed to borrow paintings for the White House. They would be hung at night, shortly before Inauguration Day.

Late in the afternoon she was driven to the West Side of Manhattan, to a large building where Strategic Transport, a branch of Strategic

Services, was building a small fleet of presidential cars and SUVs, as it was time to replace many of the old ones. She sat in the rear of a limousine and chose places for the controls she would use, then looked at leathers for the interior.

She finished her day at Frederic Fekkai's salon, where a mani/pedi technician, a facialist, and a makeup artist did their work, then ceded her to the man himself.

She arrived back at Stone's house to find him in his office, where she joined him for a drink.

"You look wonderfully refreshed. Tell me about your day," he said, and she did, in more detail than he had bargained for.

"What are we doing for dinner?"

"You are making your Manhattan restaurant debut at Patroon, with Dino, Viv, and me, at eight o'clock."

"Well, I guess it had to come sometime. Will there be photographers and all that?"

"Not unless some staffer squeals," Stone said. "I think it will be pretty quiet."

She looked at her watch. "I want an hour's nap. Then I'll freshen up, change, and be ready at a quarter to eight."

"I'll be upstairs in time to change. I'll wake you up."

"Be gentle, I've had a long day."

They arrived at Patroon on time, to be greeted by the owner, Ken Aretsky, who led them to a corner table, through a standing ovation from the other diners, many of them with phone cameras.

"Well," she said, "**that's** never happened before."

"Get used to it," Dino said.

Viv demanded a recounting of her day's events, so Stone and Dino had to amuse each other until the women had finished.

Stone was signing the check when Bill Wright appeared. "Ma'am, we'll be leaving by another door," he said.

"Is anything wrong?" Holly asked.

"No, ma'am, it's just that the second seating is arriving, and the front vestibule is very crowded with people checking their coats."

Holly and Stone exchanged a glance. "All right," she said. "Let's go."

They rose and were led to the rear of the restaurant, then through the kitchen, and out a door where deliveries arrived. Their cars were waiting there, so they said good night to the Bacchettis and got into the Bentley.

The agent shut their door, then got into the front passenger seat. "Go," he said, and they drove away faster than Stone had expected.

"All right, Bill," Holly said. "What's happened?"

"We've had a tip that something might have been planned for this evening."

"A tip from where?"

"It was anonymous, a woman, who said we should be very careful this evening."

"Were you able to trace the call?"

"Only partly. It was made from somewhere in northern Virginia, and they had Mr. Barrington's private number."

Holly sat back and exhaled. "Home, please."

Fred managed to get the garage door open at the moment they drove in, then quickly closed it.

"That's a relief," Holly said.

"It was probably nothing," Bill said, opening her door, "but we won't count on that."

Holly came to bed in a flimsy red nightgown, which Stone made disappear.

CHOPPY WATER

"I thought about this while I was having my hair and nails done," she said, receiving him.

"Well," Stone said, "there was nothing else to think about, was there?"

"Tomorrow I'll start thinking about saving the world," she said.

15

olly arrived at her new transition office at nine AM sharp. Her key staff were gathered around a plywood conference table in a back room. They stood and gave her a round of applause.

"All right," Holly said. "It's time to put aside the golden memories of all those halcyon days during the campaign and get to work." She took a file folder from her large purse, then extracted a single sheet of paper and handed it to a volunteer. "Make a dozen copies, pronto, then distribute them.

"Now, before we start the process of staffing up, let's talk about the inner circle. That would be all of you."

The volunteer returned with the copies and distributed them. "Each of you will find your name on this list and, beside it, the position on the White House staff you are being offered. You and I have been having this discussion, off and on, since before I announced my run, so there should be no surprises. That list is comprised of my final decisions. If you want the job, write me a brief letter accepting, and don't get mushy about it. At the bottom of the page is a list of key jobs as yet unfilled. I want recommendations for those slots before the day is out.

"Now, let's turn to the cabinet." She found another sheet of paper in her file, handed it to the volunteer to also be copied, then distributed.

"You will note that only one or two positions have a single name beside it. Those decisions are made. What I want from you—again, before the day is out—is one or, at the outside, two recommendations for the other departments or agencies, along with about half a page on each, saying why."

The process was repeated with the positions and names of military officers for the Joint Chiefs of Staff and the secretaries of the various armed services.

"There is a much longer list of judicial appointments to go through, and I'd like any suggested additions or subtractions by the end of the week.

There are five names, three of them women, who are being considered for the Supreme Court, when vacancies arise. Any further additions from you should be limited to one person each, with a short description of why. No disquisitions, please." She gave her file to Vice President–elect Sam Meriwether. "Sam, after you've felt out the chosen few, please write letters for my signature, dated January 20, formally offering them the jobs, and have them hand delivered on that date. We'll already know who has accepted, of course, but I can't make the appointments official until after I've taken the oath."

They worked on throughout the day, had pizza delivered for lunch, and beers for after six PM.

Holly arrived back at Stone's house at six-thirty and found Stone, and a bottle of Knob Creek, in his study. He was pouring her one as she entered the room. Bill and Claire were there, too.

Holly raised her glass. "Your continued health," she said.

"Holly," Stone interjected. "Bill and Claire are here to talk about **your** continued health."

"Am I looking a little peaked?" she asked.

"No, ma'am," Bill and Claire said, simultaneously.

Then Bill continued, "The threat last evening was not a hoax. The call came from an actual phone booth—one of the last extant, I suppose—at a convenience store and diner in Fairfax County, Virginia. The woman who made it was observed by a clerk inside to have driven away in a newish pickup truck of a dark color. Two hours after that, about the time you reached this house after dinner, an attempt was made to break into your Georgetown house. Shots were exchanged with our agents on duty there, none of them were wounded. They believe they shot one of the two intruders in the upper left arm as they fled on foot, at first, then in a newish pickup truck of a dark color, driven by a woman. The pickup truck was found, wiped clean, half an hour later. So they switched vehicles, and we have no idea to what kind."

"It sounds as though we have a friendly snake in a nest of vipers," Holly said.

"If so," Bill said, "one who has put herself at risk twice: once making the call, the other when driving away with the perpetrators."

"Let's see if we can think of a way of encouraging her, without getting her killed."

97

"We're working on that, but no joy yet. Her safety will be our primary concern."

"I should think," Stone said quietly, "that Holly's safety would be your first concern."

"Of course. I misspoke."

"I understand, Bill," Holly added. "I suppose the Georgetown incident indicates that they didn't know I wasn't still there."

"Yes, but it's unlikely that they don't know that now. Unfortunately, the tabloids have reported your presence at Bloomingdale's."

"But not at any other location?"

"No. We think this indicates a Bloomie's employee on the payroll of a newspaper."

"Has anyone in the media learned where the transition office is?"

"So far, so good," Claire said. "Oh, they'll eventually figure it out: some reporter will spot a staffer on the street and follow her there— something like that. I suggest that you make a point of going there as infrequently as possible."

"And you may as well say it, Claire," Stone said. "Back to Washington as soon as possible."

"That would be our preference," Claire said, "but we understand fully, ma'am, that you have things to do that can only be done in New York."

"Quite right," Holly replied, shooting a sidewise

glance at Stone. "You'll be happy to know that, after my shopping spree, I'll be doing all my fittings and further appointments here in Stone's house. He's kindly provided a large room upstairs where those can take place."

Bill let out a deep breath. "That was a sigh of relief, ma'am," he said. "I think it would be best if they not enter the house through the front door or the office entrance. We would prefer to meet them at the rear gate to the gardens, on Second Avenue. We have someone there."

"A good move," Stone said.

"Some of these people, like Ralph Lauren, are VIPs in their own right, and I'd prefer it if they could enter and leave through the garage."

"A touch of the cloak-and-dagger," Stone said. "They'll like that. But please let them know not to arrive in stretch limos; that would strain our facilities, not to mention our garage doors."

"I'll see to it," Bill said.

The two agents tossed off the remainder of their drinks and excused themselves.

16

Colonel Wade Sykes sat in a rear treatment room at a veterinarian's office a few miles from his base and watched the DVM inject a man's left arm with lidocaine, then flush the wound, and after testing for numbness, used a probe to locate the bullet. When he had done so, he used another tool to extract it and dropped it into a steel tray. He flushed the wound again and applied a coagulant, then trimmed the edges, stitched it closed, and bandaged it. "Okay, you can sit up now or, if you're feeling ill, just lie there for a few minutes."

"He doesn't feel ill," Sykes said. "Let's go, kid. We've got to get out of here before daylight comes."

He handed the DVM ten folded hundreds. "It was our lucky day, Doc, when you grabbed that nurse's ass and got drummed out of med school for your trouble."

"Maybe my lucky day, too. My work here is easier, and my patients don't complain. Let this guy rest for twenty-four hours, Colonel, before you put him in harm's way again." He gave the man another injection of something, then handed him an unmarked bottle of pills. "One, twice a day, until they're all gone."

"Is there a painkiller in there?" the colonel asked.

"There is not. I know your policy on pain. Those are an antibiotic. You don't want the trouble of an infected patient."

"He's going to get back on that pony pretty soon," Sykes shot back, slapping the young man on the back and causing him to wince. "C'mon, boy." He led the man outside and put him in the rear seat of his pickup, then drove off toward home.

Once there, he put the man on a bed in the bunkhouse, threw a blanket over him, and went home for dinner. His cook, an older black man named Elroy, a fine practitioner of the old Southern school, set down a plate filled with a fried chicken breast, collard greens, and creamed corn. A plate of biscuits followed, then he poured a glass of a wine his boss had already chosen. Two of Sykes's men and a young woman called Bess were waiting for him.

"How's he doing?" the woman asked.

"We don't discuss business at table," Sykes replied, rolling his eyes toward Elroy. They all continued eating in silence. When they were done they left the dirty dishes for Elroy, then adjourned to the living room, where Sykes poured everyone a brandy.

"Sorry about that, Colonel," Bess said. "I thought you trusted Elroy."

"I'm alive because there exists only a very short list of those I find trustworthy. Elroy's not very bright, and obviously he's . . . not one of us. Who knows what hatreds he harbors?"

"Quite right," she said. "Now, how is the boy?"

"He's asleep. The doctor gave him something, I think, and his wound has been properly treated. He's going to experience some pain when he wakes up, but that will be good for him. Up until today, he was a raw recruit, but tonight, he was blooded." He took a sip of his brandy. "Now," he said. "I want a proper report."

One of the men leaned forward in his chair. "Bess drove us to within a block of the house.

We took a turn around the place and found it mostly dark, with a lamp on here and there. We found a window with no alarm module on it and broke a pane. The boy was halfway through when I heard the shot from inside and saw the flash. The boy fell into my arms, and I fired two rounds to keep the on-duty man away from the window. Bess was there in a hurry, and we beat it out of there. We drove back to where we had left the van, and Bess got a combat bandage on the boy's arm, while I wiped down the pickup, then we got the hell out of there."

"Sounds like Bess is the only one of you with any brains," the colonel said.

His man flushed and sat back in his chair, silent now.

"It's obvious now that Ms. Barker was not in residence," Bess said. "She must have got out Sunday or Monday, probably after dark. A New York City newspaper put her at Bloomingdale's yesterday morning. We need better intelligence than this, Colonel. We shouldn't be reading about it in the **New York Post**."

Sykes took that as a rebuke and glowered a bit. "We're working on it."

"Best thing would be a Secret Service agent, maybe one who's recently retired or fired; somebody with an axe to grind," Bess said. "Just knowing their procedures better would be a big help."

"Don't you think I know that?" Sykes shot back.

"I don't see much evidence that you do," she said coolly. "After the cockup in Maine, we need people who can, at the very least, read a map."

"We're working on a retired agent," Sykes said.

"What are his particulars?"

"Been with the Service for twenty-two years, the last three or four becoming progressively marginalized. His wife died—a woman he hated, by all accounts—but it still threw him. I've got a man drinking with him two or three nights a week at his local pub. He's finding it hard to stretch his pension to cover his expenses."

"He sounds ideal," Bess said. "Do you want me to see him and observe?"

"Maybe," the colonel replied. "Maybe soon. I could use another opinion."

"Wire up your man, and I can nurse a drink at another table and hear their conversation. I'd like to question him, but I suppose it's too soon for that."

"Maybe not," Sykes said. "We'll see."

They finished their brandy and departed the house for bed, except for Bess, who had a guest

104

room upstairs, to keep the men away from her, or, perhaps, vice versa.

Sykes performed his bedtime ablutions, then got into the pajamas under his pillow and had his nighttime think.

Bess was on the cheeky side, but he put up with it because she was the smartest member of his group, and he did not necessarily exclude himself from that assessment. He had met her on a firing range in D.C., where she worked as a personal assistant to somebody important at Justice, and thus had had a proper vetting, which cut down on the work he otherwise would have had to pay for.

After they put away their weapons, Sykes had approached her in the small coffee bar. "Can I get you something?" he had asked.

"Thank you, a double espresso."

"No sweetener?"

"No."

He got one for each of them. "May I join you?"

"Sure."

She was fairly good-looking: slim, with nice breasts—he liked that. She looked as though she would clean up nice, so she might be a good candidate to accompany him to one of those dinner parties he kept getting invited to since his wife had left him four years ago, a year before she died.

He had not been broken up about that, since he had contrived for her benefits from the divorce to die with her, keeping him twice as rich as he otherwise would have been. Then, because she had not updated her will, he had inherited the house and property that had belonged to her father, where he now lived and ran his group.

"What do you do? Something in government, I would imagine."

"You have a good imagination," she had replied. "I'm assistant to the deputy director for criminal investigations."

Oh, good, he had thought.

17

Colonel Sykes didn't broach political views on that first occasion, and neither did Bess. By the time he had gotten around to that they had had three or four dinners. He had not made a move of any kind, but he had done his research. He knew what she earned at Justice, that she shared a small apartment with an older woman, and best of all, that she felt her job was a dead end, and she had another fifteen years before she could retire on her pension.

Then one evening she seemed a little depressed, and he gently asked her why.

"My boss won a case today, one that should have never been prosecuted."

"What sort of case?"

"You've probably read about it in the **Post**," she said. "A kid was stopped for a broken taillight, the police found an illegal gun and white-supremacist pamphlets in his car."

"I don't read the **Post**," he replied. "I like my news unfiltered by the liberal press."

"So do I, but I have to read it for work."

"What did this kid get?"

"He hasn't been sentenced yet, but my boss is recommending eight to twelve, out in six, if he keeps his nose clean and his mouth shut."

"Who is he?"

"Willard Simmons."

He slid his card across the table. "I may be able to help. Can you get me a copy of his file and his presentencing investigation and the name of the judge?"

She looked at him closely. "You? How could you help?"

"You didn't answer my question."

"Yes, I'll get you the file. A thumb drive okay?"

"Fine."

"You didn't answer my question, either."

"It's better if you don't know now. Maybe later."

She reached into her purse and came up with a thumb drive. "I was taking this home for myself, but you can have it. The judge is Stanton Rutledge."

Sykes slipped the drive into his pocket.

She seemed to look at him with new interest.

Sykes went home and plugged the thumb drive into his computer. The boy was Willard Simmons—he knew that from Bess. He was twenty-four, had two years of college at Georgetown, had been kicked out over an incident involving a racial slur, followed by a fistfight.

He knew something about the judge, too: from an old Virginia family, once considered for a slot on the federal bench, until the newspapers had published a college yearbook with a photograph of him in blackface at a frat party. He and Sykes belonged to the same club in D.C. and had met a couple of times. There was something else, too. He fished a copy of the club's monthly newsletter out of a pigeonhole in his desk and scanned it. Yes, there it was.

It was not hard to find Judge Rutledge in the early evenings, since each day he devoted an hour to relaxation in the club's bar, followed by dinner in the dining room. The judge was a widower and had no one to go home to.

Sykes got a drink from the bar and turned to find the judge at a nearby table. He strolled over. "Good evening, Judge," he said.

"Hello there, Sykes. Join me?"

"Thank you, I will." He sat down. "Can I get you the other half of that?" He nodded at the judge's nearly empty glass.

"Don't mind if you do. It's bourbon. Doesn't matter what kind."

Sykes raised a finger to a waiter. "A Knob Creek on the rocks for the judge, please."

The drink was there in a flash, and the judge took a sip. "Why, that's remarkable. What is it again?"

Sykes told him, and the judge made a note.

There was a copy of the club newsletter on the table between them. Sykes picked it up and pretended to scan it. "I see there's a Rutledge who has been proposed for membership. Any relation?"

"Yes, my nephew, Carter. He's just moved up from Richmond to take a job at State. Doesn't know all that many people in town."

Sykes slid his card across the table. "E-mail me his CV, and I'll be glad to put something together."

"That's very decent of you, Colonel."

"Not at all. Someone I didn't know was kind enough to write a letter for me, some years back. Now I can pass on the favor."

They chatted on amiably for a few minutes. Sykes had hoped the judge might bring up the case, but he didn't. So he made his own move. "Didn't I see in the **Post** that you heard the case of this young man, Simmons?"

"Yes, a tragedy at his age."

"It read like nothing more than a young man's high jinks," Sykes said. "Has he been sentenced?"

"Next Monday. The DA wants eight to twelve."

"Whew! That's mean! Does the prosecutor have some personal interest in the case?"

"I don't believe so, but he came to Justice from the ACLU. I had the feeling he was personally offended by what the boy had done." The judge looked around to be sure they were out of other members' hearing range. "The attorney general is Jewish, you know."

Sykes nodded sagely. "What a shame. I know some of the boy's folks down in my neck of the woods, and they're fine people to a man. He's the sort of young fellow I'd offer a job to when he's out."

"Really?"

"Really, Judge. I think justice should be merciful, when possible, not just mean."

"That's my philosophy, too. I'm going to read his record again, see what I can do."

"God bless you," Sykes said. "You're a humanitarian, Judge."

The judge waved off the compliment. "One does what one can."

A few days later, Sykes asked Bess to dinner again.

"Did you see the papers today?" she asked.

"No."

"The Simmons boy got time served and four years of probation. My boss was beside himself!"

"Sometimes justice does prevail," Sykes said.

"Did you have anything to do with that?"

"I ran into the judge at a club we both belong to, and we had a drink. I offered to write a letter to the admissions committee on behalf of his nephew, who is a candidate for membership. The judge asked if there was anything he could do for me." He shrugged. "I guess he wasn't just saying that."

"You are wonderful," she said, squeezing his arm.

18

Holly had spent a week in New York with Stone when they were dining with the Bacchettis at Rotisserie Georgette, an East Side restaurant specializing in roasted fowl.

"I've got to stop living as if I'm on the lam," Holly said, broaching a new subject.

"Is that how you feel at my house?" Stone asked.

"It's nothing to do with you or your house," she replied. "When I've taken office I'll be surrounded by all the security my government can manage. But right now I'm a president-in-waiting, and I don't want to make presidential demands. Also, from now until my inauguration, I don't want to be seen as hiding from the public. It would seem cowardly somehow, and that is just not in my nature. I'm my father's daughter."

Holly had been raised as an Army brat by a mostly single parent, a rawhide-tough master sergeant whose wife had died young, moving every few years and attending a dozen schools. She had never allowed anybody to bully her, and she wasn't going to start now.

Dino spoke up. "How are those two Secret Service agents at the table behind you going to take that?"

"I don't mind them two at a time," Holly replied, "but the other six scattered around the restaurant and in the vehicles outside are just too much. I've already gotten six of them killed, and I don't want their replacements living in danger because of me."

"All right," Stone said. "If that's how you're going to handle this, there are some things you need to do."

"Tell me," she replied.

"The Secret Service will take care of that. They'll explain why they are necessary to your continued survival."

"I'm not really that vulnerable," she said.

"What would have happened if you and I had

not been out sailing when the attack on Islesboro occurred?"

"We would have shot it out with them."

"I remind you that two of the dead were guarding the front and rear doors of my house. A couple of armor-piercing rounds would have taken us out as we stood by the living room fireplace, warming our hands. Fortunately, they didn't know how hardened the house was."

"What else? And don't dump it on the Secret Service."

"I don't want you moving out of my house," Stone said. "I know that's greedy of me, but where you're concerned I don't have any trouble being greedy. But sooner rather than later, someone in the media is going to figure out that we're shacking up, and seconds after they do, the world will know. I don't want that news competing with the reportage on your transition, and I don't want that information coloring your character."

"Then where should I live? I have an apartment in New York, but it's rented. I can't go back to Washington, because my transition office is here, and here is where I need to be."

"Move back into the Carlyle. I'll surreptitiously pay for the suite, if your transition budget can't handle it. And there are lots of ways for both of us to sneak into or out of the hotel."

"My budget can handle it," she said. "But I don't know if I can."

"You're sweet," Stone replied, "but we'll manage."

"What about after the inauguration?"

"I'm going to let you handle those arrangements," Stone said, "since you will have all the strings to pull. I can always be across the street at the Hay-Adams Hotel. I've already arranged for a long-term suite there."

Holly smiled. "I like good planning," she said. "What name is it in?"

"Well, I was going to put it in Dino's name, so if anybody found out, then he, not I, would be saddled with the attention of the media."

"Thanks a bunch," Dino said.

"From me, too," Viv added, "though it pisses me off that you would even consider that."

"It's registered to a Delaware corporation. That's the most security I can get without being appointed New York City's police commissioner or elected president."

"Are you going to have a tunnel dug to the White House?" Holly asked.

"That, too, would require presidential powers. The government has all the shovels."

"I'll look into whether I'll have the authority to call in the Army Corps of Engineers."

"We've still got Maine and Key West," Stone said, "when you can get a weekend off—as long as you don't make the trip in Air Force One. At least you don't play golf. I read somewhere that it costs three million dollars every time a president has to travel to a golf course."

"At least," Holly said. "That's why Will and Kate stopped playing. Kate told me that Will is turning a big chunk of the family farm in Georgia into a nine-hole course. He's been seen down there, driving a bulldozer."

"That's about as much fun as a boy can have," Viv said.

They were back in Stone's Bentley, driving home, when Bill, in the front passenger seat, started speaking into his fist.

"Uh-oh," Holly said.

Bill turned around. "Stone, your security system started squawking a minute ago, so we're going to take the scenic route home," he said.

The SUV in front of them started making turns, and a moment later, they were driving into Central Park.

"Central Park is closed to automobile traffic," Stone said to Bill.

"They're making an exception for us," Bill replied. "Fred, pull over here, and we'll wait for the all clear."

"Bill?" Holly asked. "Do you think it would be safe for us to take a moonlight walk in the park?"

"I don't see why not," Bill replied, "as long as you have an armed guard ahead of and behind you."

They got out of the car. "Let's go see who's awake at the zoo," Holly said. She led the way to the cages, with an occasional grunt or snort coming from somewhere.

"Isn't this lovely?" she asked.

"Not really," Stone replied. "Zoos depress me."

"Why?"

"Because they're prisons for animals," he replied. "And far from their natural homes."

"And I was going to suggest we take a bench and neck for a while."

"That works better for me if there's no scent of elephant dung in the air," Stone said.

Bill approached from behind them. "We've got the all clear at your house, Stone," he said. "Some sort of electronic glitch."

They trudged slowly back to the waiting car.

19

The black phone rang, and Elizabeth Potter jumped. She let it ring twice more while she composed herself, then picked it up. "Michael Crow's office," she said.

"What position does Mr. Crow hold?" a male voice asked.

Liz knew the voice immediately. "Mr. Crow is the deputy attorney general for criminal prosecution," she replied.

"Can we talk on this line?" he asked.

"I'm sorry, Mr. Crow is attending a meeting outside the office. May I take a message for him?"

"When do you think he could get back to me?"

"I should think between twelve-thirty and one."

He gave her a number. "I'll be waiting for the call."

She wrote down the number; probably a burner cell phone. "I'll see that he gets the message," she said, then hung up. She memorized the number, then dropped the slip of paper into her shredder, which immediately ingested it.

She waited until 12:35 before returning the call.

"Yes?"

"It's Bess."

"Ah! Where are you?"

"At a table in a courtyard near my office."

He gave her some walking directions. "It's a pub called Shannon's," he said. "Ten minutes?"

"Five," she replied. She put away her cell phone and began walking. Six minutes later she spotted the pub: not the sort that would attract anyone she knew for lunch. She found Sykes in a booth at the back. "Nice place you've got here," she said, sliding in.

"Let's just say that it doesn't attract the carriage trade."

"Nor the Justice trade."

Sykes looked around, then back at her. "Quite right. I've received word that our bird is flying back to Washington for a few days."

"That's interesting. Where will she roost?"

"Two possibilities: the residence where your friends last made contact with her, or the family quarters of a large, white residence not too far away."

Someone set a bowl of something before her. "What is this?" she asked, sniffing at it.

"Irish stew," he replied. "The best in town."

"How much competition is there?"

"Perhaps a dozen or so such pubs."

She tasted it gingerly. "Not too bad."

"Would you like something else?"

"What would you suggest?"

"Well, the **drisheen** has been praised by connoisseurs."

"What is that?"

"Stomach of cow," he replied, "sliced, seasoned, cooked, and cut into bite-sized pieces."

"The Irish stew sounds delicious," she said, filling a spoon and eating it.

"A wise choice," Sykes said. "What do you think about our problem?"

"Well, let's see: the last location has probably been fortified since our last visit."

"Probably so."

"And the alternative is guarded by a tall fence, dogs, guards armed with automatic weapons, and ground-to-ground missiles on the roof. Does either option sound inviting?"

"They both have the attraction of unexpected-ness, one having been previously visited, the other suffering from complacency."

"'Complacency'? You think so?"

"I guess that means the previous location."

"Not unless you can get someone inside, unde-tected, long enough to plant explosives," she said. "And that someone will not be me."

"I thought you bolder," he said.

"Foolish, more likely."

He reached out, stroked her forearm, and took her hand.

"Never that," he said.

"Colonel," she said, withdrawing her hand, "there is something you should know about me before we continue this conversation."

"That you're beautiful? I already know that."

"That I'm a lesbian," she replied.

He withdrew his hand as if her flesh were afire. "I would never have guessed," he managed to say, finally.

"That's the way I prefer it," she said. "I'm afforded a wider range of company, if no one suspects."

"Oh?"

"Most people are distrustful of others who present themselves as one thing, then turn out to be another. I find it more useful to let them make their presumptions, then follow their pre-conceived notions."

"What would you say if another woman asked you directly: 'Are you a lesbian?'"

"I would reply, 'Why? Are you?' And if she answered honestly in the affirmative, I would consider her as a potential lover. Men and women are not so different in the manner of their choices, as long as they're on familiar ground."

"And how long have you been, ah, that way?"

"You're so delicate, Sykes. Since birth, probably before. It's not a choice, you know. Just as you didn't choose to be heterosexual."

"That's very enlightening," Sykes said.

"I'm so happy you find it to be."

"Now, back to the reason for our meeting."

"Ah, yes. Can you present me with a more opportune setting?"

"Not yet."

"Colonel, I seem to recall someone at your dinner table saying that your intelligence was inadequate."

"I'm working on it. Do you, at your place of work, have access to the file of Holly Barker?"

"I do, if the file includes behavior indicating criminal activity or proclivity. I hardly think, given the positions she has held, that she had anything of the sort in her background. If so, it would have been discovered long ago."

"Nevertheless, I'd like to know if she has a file and, if so, what's in it."

"If I can find a plausible excuse to work late one evening soon, then I know where the key is kept."

"How about this evening?"

"Tomorrow evening would be better."

"Call me the day after," he said, hipping his way out of the booth. "Lunch is on me." He walked out of the pub.

She didn't watch him go.

20

Sykes felt a little sick to his stomach. He had been fantasizing about being in bed with her, but he wanted no part of a woman who wasn't attracted to him as a man. She could still be useful, though; she was bright, brave, and willing to take risks. Maybe she would even turn up some information from those Justice files.

Elizabeth went back to her office. "Do you have an Alka-Seltzer?" she asked her secretary as she passed her desk.

"Sure," the woman said, digging in a desk drawer and coming up with a packet.

Elizabeth dropped the two disks into half a glass of water, then watched them fizz. She drank down the bubbly stuff, burped, and rinsed the glass. Nearly instant relief from the stew, as promised.

She opened her safe and found the key to the secure file room, where old papers were kept. She went to the B drawer and looked for Barker, Holly, then took it back to her desk and started at the beginning. It made interesting reading.

Holly had been raised on Army bases in the States and in Germany. Her mother died during a flu epidemic in Germany, when the child was eight. When she was in high school her father had written to a Florida congressman, requesting an appointment to West Point for his daughter, enclosing a transcript of her high school studies. He received a negative form-letter reply, so young Holly joined the Army, excelled in basic and advanced training, and enrolled at the University of Maryland, which offered a degree program for serving soldiers. She got her bachelor's degree in two and a half years, then applied for Officer Candidate School and was rejected. Her father wrote a letter to a man he had served under, who had known Holly as a teenager on the Army base in Mannheim, and who, by then, was a brigadier general. Holly was duly accepted into the next class at OCS.

Upon graduation, at the head of her class, she had applied for Intelligence but was passed over and offered the military police. In the MPs she consistently received outstanding fitness reports and was promoted as quickly as the rules allowed, rising to command an MP company, then, as a major, to executive officer of a regiment. There her progress ended.

She was drugged and raped by the colonel who was her commanding officer. She filed a criminal complaint, along with another young woman, a sergeant, who had suffered the same experience with the man. The colonel was found not guilty by a panel of his fellow officers, and Holly received an unwanted transfer to a transportation company. It was then that she had read, in a law enforcement magazine, an ad for an assistant chief of police in a small Florida town, Orchid Beach. She applied and was hired. She excelled, as she had in everything she had ever done. A year later, her chief died, and she applied for his job. She got the job on a trial basis.

As chief she became aware of possible criminal activity at a real-estate development where all of the homeowners had questionable backgrounds.

She contacted the FBI, who took over her investigation. But she had continued to work on it almost to the exclusion of everything else. An agent of the CIA turned up and helped her: first, to break the case without the help of the FBI, and then to join the Agency as a raw recruit sent for training to Fort Peary, known as the Farm.

She progressed through the CIA, becoming an assistant to the then deputy director, Lance Cabot, and later to Katharine Rule, who later had become Katharine Lee and the president of the United States.

Now, after two terms as Kate Lee's secretary of state, Holly Barker was the president-elect of the United States.

But something small in her record caught Elizabeth's eye. The colonel who was charged with her rape had retired from the Army and was hired as the chief of police in Orchid Beach, while Holly was still serving in that role on a trial basis. She must have been furious, Elizabeth thought. But then, not long after his arrival in the small town, the colonel committed suicide.

Elizabeth got on her computer and began researching the colonel's case. All the evidence in the case supported suicide as the cause of death, except the absence of a motive. Holly was soon given the chief's job. A suspicious person, as Elizabeth was, might think that Holly Barker had a perfectly evident motive for murder, and the skills to leave no evidence at the scene. She did, however, have an alibi; she had been having a drink at a local bar with another police officer. Easily arranged, Elizabeth thought, if the other officer shared her opinion of the dead colonel.

Elizabeth began checking on the history of the officer who had provided the alibi: killed in the line of duty two years later, while investigating a case of domestic violence, well after Holly had left for her CIA training. Dead end.

Elizabeth closed and locked away the file, feeling relieved that she had found nothing to sully the name of a woman she admired. Still, it might stir up Sykes.

21

Sykes had all four of his men and one woman, Bess Potts, to dinner on a Saturday night. They dined on porterhouse steaks, perfectly grilled and sliced by Elroy Hubbard, who had been cooking for him for the past four months.

"Where did you find Elroy?" Bess asked Sykes.

Sykes poured her more of the grand California cabernet. "He was a ship's cook in the Navy for more than twenty years. When a lot of the older ships were cut up for scrap, and he found himself ashore, his former CO on a battleship got him transferred to Naval Air Station Pensacola, as chef in the officers club. When he finally retired, a naval acquaintance of mine recommended him."

"He's just perfect, isn't he?" she asked.

"Just about," Sykes replied.

"But he seems not to have your full confidence," Bess said. "Last time I was here, you had a tendency to change the subject when he was nearby. Is it a racial thing?"

"I guess I'm as much a racist as the next man," Sykes said. "He's always had a bit of an attitude that troubled me."

"I see," she said. "After dinner I'd like to talk to you about something I found in the files at Justice."

"Oh, good."

When the others returned to their quarters, Bess hung back, then produced a copy of Holly Barker's file. "I think you'll find this interesting," she said.

"Do you mind if I read it now?" Sykes asked.

"Go right ahead."

Sykes read the file rapidly, then looked up from his brandy. "This thing about her chief's suicide is interesting, isn't it?"

"I think so, too. She had the skills and training to shoot him with his own gun, clean up after herself, and leave the body to be found the following morning by his maid."

"She had an alibi, too," Sykes said.

"Yes, and it stood up. The man who said he was with her in a bar died in the line of duty at a later time."

"You think she killed the colonel?"

"She certainly had an excellent motive, didn't she? Drugged and raped, then he's found not guilty by a jury that included a buddy of his."

"Was there a tox screen on the body of her former CO?"

"There was an autopsy, but the local ME didn't think a tox screen was indicated. And the body was cremated. I tried to search the records of the drugstore where he had his prescriptions filled, but they were dumped a long time ago."

"So here's a headline for you: PRESIDENT-ELECT A SUSPECT IN A COP MURDER AND FAKED SUICIDE. COP'S MEDICAL RECORDS VANISHED."

"Pretty good," she said, "but not all his medical records, just his prescriptions."

"Picky, picky, picky," Sykes said. "I know a fellow with a radio talk show who's really good at turning a news story into a walking, talking myth, and he has an audience who'll eat it up."

"That sounds like Jake Wimmer," she said.

"You're absolutely right," Sykes said.

"It's a little late, isn't it? She's already been elected."

"It's not too late to make her life hell for a while," Sykes said, "and it could come back to bite her in the ass when she's running for reelection."

"You don't want it traced back to you," Bess said. She hadn't counted on this.

"Jake knows when to talk and when not to talk," Sykes said. "And if he should talk, he knows how to blame the right people."

"You'd better be very, very careful," Bess said. "You might get more than your fingers burned." She tossed back her brandy and got up. "Time for me to go," she said. "I don't need a hangover tomorrow morning." She thanked him for dinner, found her coat, and drove away from the house.

All the way home she thought about what she had done, and the possibility of unintended consequences. She was going to have to find a way to turn this back onto Sykes.

At home, she sat down and made a list of people to contact, especially people in the printed press and the television political shows.

Then she sat down at her typewriter and wrote a description of what she had seen in Holly Barker's file and what Sykes's reaction was when he read it, then she faxed it to a contact.

That was all she could do for now.

22

When Elizabeth arrived at her desk on Monday morning, there was an encrypted e-mail waiting for her. She ran the app, then read the message. Alfresco lunch today? 12:30? She responded: OK.

She bought a deli sandwich at noon, then drove to Rock Creek Park and left her car in a legal space. She walked down a trail and found a picnic table; he was already there.

He rose to greet her, a cool handshake. "Have a seat," he said.

They both opened their bags and began eating their sandwiches.

"Is anything wrong?" she asked.

"I'm concerned by your lack of progress," he said.

She frowned. "What more do you expect me to do?"

"I want you to tie Sykes and his cohorts to the shootings of the Secret Service agents in Maine."

"Well, I know that, but I can't find a provable connection."

"Have you found a connection that you can't prove?"

"No, no connection at all; only the visit to the Georgetown house."

"That's breaking and entering with a deadly weapon at best," he said.

"Do you think I don't know that?"

"I know you know it."

"There's something else you should know about, though." She handed him the passage from the Barker file, and he read it.

"So what?" He handed it back to her.

"I may have made an error in judgment," she said.

"How so?"

"My hope was that reading it might jolt Sykes into talking about her, telling me more. Instead, it may have set off something that could be difficult to control."

"Tell me everything."

She did, and when she was finished neither of them said anything for a while.

"You're right," he said. "This could open a can of worms we don't want to go near. That guy, Wimmer, is a rumor machine. This will end up on Fox News as a conspiracy theory that could be difficult to handle, and for years to come."

"I had hoped that you might be able to think of a way to turn this around on Sykes and Wimmer before they can propagate it," she said.

"Have you thought of anything?"

"Yes, but I don't have the contacts to pull it off."

"Pull what off?"

"I had thought we might get this story out in some more conventional medium, maybe a newspaper interview."

"You mean if Barker brings it up in an interview, and it's published, it might negate Wimmer's efforts?"

"Yes, then she could say, 'That's hardly a surprise. I already spoke with a journalist about it in an interview. It doesn't surprise me that Wimmer would try to twist it, though.'"

He thought about that for a moment. "Disarm their weapon, so to speak?"

"Exactly. Do you know someone, a journalist, who could help?"

"I know someone who could accomplish that, as long as she didn't know we were using her as a counter to Wimmer."

"Who's that?"

"Do you know Peg Parsons?"

"I read her column, but I've never met her. I take it you have."

"Yes, we had a thing for a few months in college, but it was a long time ago, and it didn't last."

"Would she be glad to hear from you?"

"That's the thing. I don't know."

"It couldn't hurt to try, could it?"

"I don't know that, either. If it went wrong, it might make things worse."

"Well, I don't have any other ideas nearly as good as this. It's worth trying."

"If I can handle it."

"Look, why don't you just swear her to secrecy and tell her the whole story?"

"That might screw it up."

"Wouldn't it be worse to lie to her, then have her catch on?"

"She'd be furious, in that case."

"I say it's worth a try."

"That would amount to recruiting her."

"I think she'd think it amounts to a scoop," Elizabeth said.

"Let me think about it. There's my wife to consider, too."

"How does your wife come into it?"

"If she that heard Peg and I saw each other, she'd go right through the roof. I made the mistake of telling her that we had been fucking at Georgetown, and she sort of grinds her teeth when she hears Peg's name."

"Then you're going to have to be up front with your wife, too," Elizabeth said.

"That's easier said than done," he replied.

"Tom, are you afraid of your wife?"

"You're damned right I am. You don't know her; she has a bad temper when she's riled, and a violent streak, too. She broke one of my teeth with a wine bottle once."

"Well, if you're contemplating divorce, here's your chance," Elizabeth said.

"Maybe," he said, "if I can convince her up front that it's a matter of national security . . ."

"Tom, how did you ever get to be an assistant director of the FBI? You're afraid of your own wife!"

"I can't deny that," he said.

"Look, here's how to handle her." Elizabeth outlined a plan.

"And part of it is, I have to be mad at **her**?"

"You'll be mad at her, because her attitude is forcing you to tell her about a top secret op, just to placate her in advance."

"I'm not sure I'm that good an actor," he replied.

"Well, there's no time to send you to the Actors Studio for training."

"They didn't cover this at Quantico," he said.

"They covered undercover, didn't they?"

"Yeah."

"Look at this as if you're going undercover as yourself."

He burst out laughing.

"Is it such a crazy idea?"

"It is a crazy idea, but it might work."

"Don't overthink it. You have to be real."

"She's real enough for both of us," he said.

"Just get it done." She wadded up her paper bag and took aim at a waste bin.

Tom took it out of her hand. "I'll dispose of this," he said.

"We're leaving no trace, huh?"

"Exactly."

23

Tom Blake left the J. Edgar Hoover building and drove to his house in Georgetown.
As he opened the garage door with the remote and pulled inside, he was grateful—as he was every time he came home—to his late father-in-law.

There was some discomfort about living in such a fine old house in such a beautiful neighborhood: he had had to explain to a committee of agency accountants how he could afford to live in a better house than the director. None of them, apparently, had received such a wedding gift. And they had gone over the deeds and closing documents carefully.

Tom also had had to get used to having a wife who earned three times more than he did—and that was before her father died and she took over his large insurance agency and got a big raise.

He switched off the car and sat in it for a couple of minutes, working up a head of steam. If this were a play, the stage direction for this scene would read: ENTER, ANNOYED.

He found her in the kitchen, as usual. One of her great marital attributes was that she cooked beautifully and loved doing it. He had a constant battle with his waistline. He nearly lost his worked-up annoyance when he saw that she was wearing a frilly apron and nothing else. This was one of her little invitations to have sex, and she didn't care if it was on the kitchen island. That was fine with him, too, even if he had to watch out for the hanging copper pots.

"Good evening," he said, more formally than usual. She froze for a moment, then turned slowly around, her bare breasts struggling for freedom from the apron. "And what, exactly, do you mean by that?" she asked.

"I have a big problem," he said, "and you're the cause of it."

She frowned. Her interest in immediate sex went out of her eyes. "Go on, tell me."

"A big part of my problem is that I can't tell you," he replied. "It's a matter of national security."

"Well, that's a new one," she said.

"There's something I have to do, and you can't know about it."

"Why won't you tell me?"

"I didn't say I won't tell you. I said you can't know about it. Think about that for a minute."

She thought about it, and her face relaxed. "Oh, I think I see. You're going to tell me, and then I have to forget about it."

"You won't have anything to forget," he said.

"All right, you're going to tell me, but I can't know."

"You're starting to grasp the situation."

"But if that's the case, why tell me about it at all?"

"Because I can't lie to you."

"Tommy," she said. "Have you been fucking somebody else?"

"I have not, and I have no intention of doing so."

She stared at him. "You're waiting for me to insist that you tell me," she said.

"Something like that."

"All right, Tommy, tell me, and I'll forget I ever heard it."

"You can't say that lightly," he replied. "This is

the equivalent of swearing under oath that you don't know this."

She looked around her suspiciously. "Have you had the house wired? Are we being recorded?"

"Good God, no! If I can't tell you about this, why would I want a bunch of tech guys at the Bureau to know about it?"

"All right, I'm ready to forget I ever heard it. Go."

"The worst part first."

"I'm ready."

"I have to have lunch, maybe even dinner, with Peg Parsons."

"You tricked me!" she shouted.

"What?"

"You tricked me into giving you permissions to fuck Peg Parsons! Again!"

"This is why I didn't want to tell you," he said, shaking his head. "And, for the record, I haven't fucked Peg Parsons for more than twenty years."

"Some things are timeless," she replied.

"Do you want to hear why I have to see her?"

"I'm dying to hear it."

"I have to ask her to write a column using information I'm going to give her that could be construed as against the national interest."

"Do I want to know what that information is?"

"No, certainly not."

"Tell me!" She stamped her foot. This was something akin to a Spanish bull pawing the dirt in the ring.

"Many years ago Holly Barker was a police officer in a Florida town, and she was, briefly, considered a suspect in the murder of her chief, who had, some time before, drugged and raped her."

Amanda's jaw was working, but nothing was coming out. Holly Barker was her idol.

"Make me understand," she said, finally.

"Someone who is bitterly opposed to her politically intends to give this information to that creep of the airwaves, Jake Wimmer, who will fashion it into a conspiracy theory that could haunt her for years."

"Surely this was investigated at the time," Amanda said.

"It was investigated at the time by the internal affairs department of her police force, by the Florida state police—and later by the FBI and the CIA. Ms. Barker is as clean as a hound's tooth."

"But that won't matter, will it?"

Tom shook his head sadly. "No. Not to these people."

"And how does the awful Peg Parsons come into this?"

"We want her to publish the story, after having investigated it thoroughly herself. We want her to review the four earlier investigations during that process, then write a column about it. Then Wimmer's conspiracy theory will be blunted, maybe even spiked."

"Tommy," Amanda said, "I think that's just wonderful!"

"Then I can see Peg, and you'll forget about it?"

She shrugged, and one loop of her apron fell off a shoulder. "Eventually."

"Not eventually, **now**."

"All right, now."

"And you have no memory of being told?"

"None. Who do I have to fuck to prove it to you?"

"That would be me," Tom said, working on his buttons.

Amanda slithered out of the apron and met him on the kitchen island. He made the gong sound only once.

24

Bess Potts turned down the long dirt road that led to Colonel Sykes's compound. It was a winding and very pretty drive, climbing a couple of hundred feet from the highway. She pressed the down button on her window and let the sweet air in. She also let in an unexpected sound: the muffled crack of what sounded like a silenced rifle.

She pulled into the parking area outside Sykes's house, which was set in a notch of the hillside. She switched off the engine and sat in the car for a moment, waiting to hear the sound again, so she could track its location.

Her arm was resting on the car door, and

something struck her elbow. She looked at the door and found that her driver's-side mirror had disappeared. Apparently, that was what had struck her elbow.

"CEASE FIRE!" came a tinny voice from the distance, then all was quiet. "STAND DOWN!" the voice shouted.

Wade Sykes stepped from behind the house and walked over to her car. "Are you all right, Bess?" he asked.

"Weren't you expecting me?"

"Not for another quarter hour," he replied. "Do you need anything?"

"Yes, I need a new side mirror, and it's one of those smart ones, so it will be expensive."

"I'll replace it, of course. Were you hit?"

Bess unbuttoned her sleeve and rolled it up, exposing her elbow, which sported a huge lump. "Maybe an ambulance?"

Sykes opened her car door and helped her out. "I don't think we'll need an ambulance, but let's get you into the kitchen and get some ice on that."

She followed him inside, holding her elbow in her other hand. The lump had begun to throb.

"Elroy!" Sykes shouted. "Get out here!"

Slowly, Elroy Hubbard opened the swinging

door to the kitchen. "You wanted something, Colonel?"

"Get some ice on Miss Potts's elbow. She's had an accident, and it's swelling."

"Accident?" Bess asked. "Someone was shooting at me."

"My dear," Sykes said, "if Eugene had been shooting at you, we'd be calling a hearse right now."

Elroy came out of the kitchen holding a dish towel, twisting it to keep the ice in. She sat down at the dining table, gently propping her arm on it, and he applied the ice pack. "Just hold it right there with your other hand," he said gently, "and turn it every now and then to keep the cold on it."

Bess followed his instructions. "Wade, what the hell is going on out there?"

"Target practice," Sykes said. "We do a lot of that around here."

"How many visitors have you lost?" she asked, a touch of acid in her voice.

"None so far," he said. "Fortunately."

"And why is Eugene employing a silencer?"

"Why do you think that?" Sykes asked.

"Because I couldn't hear the shots, just a **pfft** sound. Ergo, a silencer. That's illegal, isn't it?"

"It's a beer can, filled with sawdust from my

woodworking shop, that's affixed to the rifle barrel with duct tape."

"I believe that's the very definition of a silencer," she said.

"How is your elbow feeling?"

"Better, sort of numb."

"The swelling will go down after a while. Would you like a drink to help it along?"

"Scotch," she said. "Rocks, too."

"I'll join you." He handed her a glass and she took a gulp of it.

"Is Eugene going to shoot it out of my hand?"

"Of course not. What happened was completely an accident."

"Or maybe Eugene doesn't like me a little."

"I expect he's sitting on his bunk, crying his eyes out as we speak," Sykes said.

She managed a chuckle. "I'm glad the mirror got in the way, or I wouldn't have an elbow."

"We use silencers for outdoor shooting to keep from disturbing the neighbors."

"What neighbors? I've never seen a living soul around here during my visits."

"Oh, we have a couple of old ladies—sisters—who live nearby. Once, they called the police when they heard gunfire."

"A perfectly normal reaction," Bess said.

"Perhaps," he replied. "But I'm building something in my shop that will be much more effective."

"Oh, good," Bess replied. "Then Eugene can pick the old ladies off their front porch and never make a sound."

Skyes managed a smile. "What a good idea. Good practice for Eugene."

"And who or what is Eugene practicing to shoot?"

"Did I say he was going to shoot somebody? That was your suggestion. Elroy, bring us a new ice pack!"

Elroy silently entered the room and exchanged a new dishcloth for the old one, then left the way he had come.

"That guy gets under my skin sometimes," Sykes grumbled.

Bess looked at him and rolled her eyes.

"Don't you worry. I always treat him with kid gloves. I wouldn't want to lose the best biscuit maker in Virginia."

"Come on, Wade. What's the silencer for?"

"You haven't been with us long enough to ask questions like that," Sykes said.

"You're right," she said sheepishly. "I apologize."

"Apology accepted."

"I suppose you're not going to need my help with that one," she said.

"Probably not. I'll let you know if that changes."

"Anything I can do," she replied.

Elroy stuck his head in past the door. "Supper's in five minutes, Colonel," he said.

"Ring the dinner bell, then," Sykes replied.

Elroy disappeared into the kitchen, and after a moment, an old-fashioned school bell began ringing.

Sykes removed the ice pack from Bess's elbow and scrutinized it. "Much improved," he said. "I think we can do away with the ice."

"Thank Eugene for not doing away with me," Bess said, tucking her napkin under her chin as the others entered and took their seats.

25

Tom Blake had only just arrived at his desk the following morning when his secretary walked in. "Yes?"

"That woman who won't give her name is on line three," she said.

"Thank you." He put his hand on the phone and looked at his secretary, waiting for her to leave. She finally got the message. He picked up the phone. "Yes?"

"I've news from the south," she said.

"What news?"

"The chief has got a man there who's a pretty good shot, and he's working on improving his performance."

"With what weapon?"

"A high-powered rifle, and the fearless leader is working on a special silencer for it."

"That sounds ominous."

"I thought so, too. Do you have her schedule?"

"She's coming back to D.C. for a few days," he said.

"Well, there you are."

"Do you really think he has the balls for that?"

"People like him don't need balls. They have fanaticism to drive them."

"A good point. We'll take steps."

"What will you do?"

"I'll call the Secret Service, of course. Protecting her is their job."

"What's your job?"

"Gathering intelligence and keeping them informed."

"I thought that was my job."

"It's **our** job. Who is the sniper?"

"His name is Eugene; I don't have a last name."

"We'll have it somewhere," Tom said. "We might even have a word with him, if the Secret Service approves."

"I wouldn't do that," she said.

He thought about it for a minute. "You're right. It might compromise you, and we wouldn't want that, would we?"

"Did you have the fight with your wife?"

"I did. Your advice was good, though, so I won. I'm having lunch with the lady in question today."

"Be careful you don't tell her too much," she said.

"Just what she needs to know."

"Good luck," she said, then hung up.

Tom got there first. It was a corner table near the fireplace, and it had been swept less than an hour ago, followed by the placing of an electronic bug in the little lamp on the table. He wanted every word of their conversation; he might have to play it back for Amanda, if she became obstreperous.

Peg Parsons appeared in the doorway and spotted him immediately. She strode over to the table and stopped. "I want another table," she said.

"Why? If I'm wearing a bug, it will move with me."

"Are you wearing a bug?"

"No," he lied. "Do you see any empty tables?"

She looked around. "Now that you mention it, no."

"Then have a seat," he said. "Or would you prefer mine?"

"This one will do," she said, then sat down

opposite him. "So, Tom, how are you and what do you want?"

"Would you like a drink?"

"Love one. A prosecco, please."

Tom lifted a finger, and a waiter appeared. "One prosecco and one San Pellegrino," he said. The waiter left.

"Why aren't you having a drink?" she asked.

"FBI agents don't drink in public at lunchtime," he replied. "They might make fools of themselves."

"So your plan is to get me drunk, while you remain cool and sober."

"It's not my plan, but if it's what you feel like doing, go right ahead."

"From the door I immediately saw two senators and four congressmen," she said.

"Well spotted."

Her drink and his water arrived.

"I'm going to assume this conversation is being recorded," she said.

"Go right ahead and assume," he replied. "Are you recording it?"

"Should I?"

"Up to you, but I have to tell you first that the life of a very important person is involved."

She reached into her bag, found her iPhone, and

disabled its recording function. "There, now it's just you and me."

"That's best, I think."

"So, tell me how I would get this person killed if I blabbed?"

"Au contraire," he said, as he might have when they were in the same French class. "Blabbing is what I want from you."

"So, you want me to send a message to somebody?"

"In a manner of speaking, yes."

"Who?"

"An infamous spinner of conspiracy theories, who is one of your readers."

"Who, and how do you know he reads my stuff?"

"Jake Wimmer, because he complains about you nearly every day."

"Point taken. And what particular flea do you want me to put in his ear?"

Tom took a sheet of paper from his inside pocket and handed it to her. "This flea."

She read it. "And why didn't I know about this?"

"Because it didn't come up at her Senate hearing when she was appointed secretary of state."

"Did the president arrange for it not to come up?"

Tom gave her a big shrug. "How would I know a thing like that?"

"Did you?"

"I did not. It was thoroughly investigated by two police agencies at the time, and by the CIA and the FBI later."

"Was there even the slightest evidence that she might have shot the man and made it look like a suicide?"

"No, not a whit, and there's a reason for that."

"What reason?"

"She didn't do it, so there was no evidence that she did. She also passed two polygraph exams, at the Agency and the Bureau."

"So I'm on solid ground, if I print that."

"Granite."

"And you want me to head him off at the pass?"

"Exactly. Your piece will be on the AP, UPI, and Reuters wires before it hits the newsstands, so Wimmer is not going to waste his time inventing a conspiracy theory that's already been repeatedly debunked."

"Okay, I'm in. I'll have the duck. And after that, you want to go someplace and do something that rhymes with the dish?"

"Peg, I have a wife I love dearly, who demands all my strength at home. Also, she would cut my throat with a dull knife if she thought for a moment that I was doing that."

As he was speaking, he was giving her a thumbs-up while switching off the bug in his pocket.

26

Bill Wright got a call from his boss. "Good morning," he said.

"Bill, we got a tip from our source," the man said.

"Same one as last time?"

"Yes."

"And what good news does she have for us today?"

"The group we're dealing with has a marksman in its midst, who is undergoing further training. Also, a special silencer is being created specifically for his weapon."

"Which is?"

"We're told a high-powered rifle, that's all. No caliber or maker."

"We're sure this is the same source as last time?"

"Apparently."

"Can I ask a question?" Bill said.

"Of course."

"If our source knows who these people are, why haven't we arrested them for the Maine killings?"

"She has no knowledge of that incident and, thus, no evidence to connect them with it."

"Does she have any clue as to where or when they will make the attempt?"

"No, but the source says they know that she's coming back to Washington for a few days, so that gives us a time frame."

"I'd give a lot to know how they know that."

"We all would, Bill. Our task now is to absolutely ensure her safety while she's here. When and how is she arriving?"

"Tomorrow, aboard her friend Barrington's aircraft. At Manassas—it's a lot easier to cover than Dulles."

"It is. The equivalent of a White House detail will meet her. It's a budget-buster, but I have to do it."

"May I make a suggestion?"

"Of course."

"Instead of meeting her with a lot of agents, why don't we just disguise her a bit and have her met by a car that's armored but appears to be civilian."

"What do you mean by 'disguise'?"

"Gray wig, sunglasses, dowdy coat. Age her twenty years."

"That's unconventional for us."

"But cheap," Bill reminded him.

"I can't argue with that. You handle it from your end."

"I can do that. I have another suggestion."

"Go ahead."

"If she stays in her Georgetown house, then we're back to the full-detail problem. Why not put her in a place that's inaccessible and much safer?"

"Sounds good. What do you have in mind?"

"The family quarters of the White House."

"You think the president will go for that?"

"I think she'll be delighted. They're old friends and colleagues."

"That's right. I'll call the president."

"Why not just call the head of the White House detail and ask him to ask her? Keep it out of official channels, where it might cause talk."

"I think that's a great idea, Bill. Let me know if you have any more suggestions." He hung up.

Bill knew a retired agent who had a wife who

was a theatrical makeup artist. Her name was Tillie Marks, and he soon established contact.

"What can I do for you?" Tillie asked.

"I have a lady in my care, and we have to age her twenty years to get her safely off an airplane in plain view of others, then into a car."

"That's it?" Tillie asked.

"That's it."

"Let me make a suggestion that will save you twenty-five hundred dollars, which is my fee for a day's work."

"Please do."

"Find out her hat size, then go to Bloomingdale's and buy a gray wig, on the longer side. Put her in that, with a head scarf and sunglasses."

"Is that going to make her look twenty years older?"

"It will if you give her a walker, available at any big drugstore or medical supply store."

"Tillie, you're a peach," Bill said. "I owe you a good dinner one night soon."

"We never turn down anything free," she said, and hung up.

Claire Dunn walked into the room, and he brought her up to date.

"I can do that," she said.

"How much is a gray wig?"

"A couple hundred, maybe more. The walker won't be much."

"I want you to fly down with her and appear to be helping her off the airplane. Do it slowly, and have the car waiting at the wingtip. Then she can use the walker to hobble out there, with you beside her."

"Where's she traveling from the airport, and in what?"

"To the White House. Keep the disguise until you're on the elevator with her. I asked for a civilian-looking car, but armored."

"They've got a bunch of refurbished and beefed-up Lincoln Town Cars in the garage. That should do."

"Perfect."

"When are we leaving?"

"Ask the lady when you're getting her hat size."

"Am I going to stay with her while she's in D.C.?"

"You are, and you'll be covered by the White House detail."

"How do we get back to New York?"

"Same airplane, same airport, same car, and same disguise."

Bill's phone rang. It was his boss.

"The president would be delighted to have her as a guest. It's convenient for both of them, because our Kate is going to be conducting a tutorial for Holly, on how to be a female president. The rest is in your hands."

Bill explained what they were doing and got a hearty approval.

"And it's cheap," his boss said.

"You can add the savings to my salary," Bill said. His boss chuckled and hung up.

"Why don't you come upstairs with me," Claire said. "We'll brief her together."

27

Holly had no idea what her hat size was. "On the rare occasions when I've bought a hat, I've just tried them on until one fits. I never thought about them coming in sizes."

"Small, medium, or large?" Claire hazarded.

"I'm not a small or medium girl," Holly replied. "What am I going to wear for a coat?"

"We'll supply one from our own stock."

"You mean it will be bulletproof."

"Well, yes, but the big benefit is that it will put twenty pounds on your frame and make you look older."

"That's a benefit?"

"It is for this occasion. Once you're at the White

House, you can take it all off until the trip back to New York."

Holly sighed, then went back to work having her clothes fitted.

Claire picked up the phone, called her Washington office, and wheedled a purchase order out of someone in accounting, then called her supplier. "She's five ten or eleven, 140 pounds."

"That would be tall and slim," the man said. "How long do you want the coat?"

"Down to the mid-calf."

"Got it. Gimme till the end of the day and an address."

Claire gave him Stone's address and the purchase order number and hung up.

Ten minutes later he called back. "I've got one in stock in black. How's black?"

"Black is good."

"Bye." He hung up again.

"I heard that," Holly said. "Black isn't good for me. It makes me look like an old woman."

"That's the idea, ma'am. This is a disguise, remember?"

"Oh, yeah. I'm still in shopping mode."

"This is what we could call the fool- 'em mode. The alternative is a detail of twenty-five men with shotguns and half a dozen armored SUVs. It's expensive."

"Who's paying for this?"

"The Secret Service. We add it to our next budget request."

Stone came up from downstairs. "Lunch in ten minutes," he said. "What's going on up here?"

Claire explained the plan to him.

"Cunning," he said.

"Oh," Holly said, "bill my transition team for the airplane."

"It's free of charge," Stone said.

"No, that would be too much like graft. Then later, when you want something from me, people will say it's a payoff for the airplane."

"How much should I bill?"

"Whatever it would cost to charter the same airplane."

"You'll be shocked," he said.

She shook her head. "The Treasury will be shocked, but they'll spread the cost around, since there'll be half a dozen Secret Service people and one Air Force pilot on board."

Stone called Joan. "Please find out what it would cost to charter a Gulfstream 500 for an hour and a half flight to Manassas, Virginia, and a return flight in a few days."

"Don't you already have one of those?" Joan asked.

"Yes, but we have to figure out what to charge the transition team for it." He hung up.

"This is going to cost twenty-five thousand dollars," Holly said.

Joan rang back and told Stone the cost. He hung up. "Not even close," he said. "It's thirty-eight thousand dollars, each way."

"We need the cheapest available price," Holly said.

"That's it. Joan called three services. Not all of them have a G-500 available."

"If it were up to me, I'd hitchhike," Holly said.

"You are hitchhiking," Stone replied.

"Hitchhiking is free."

"Free ain't what it used to be," Stone pointed out. "Now come to lunch."

Lunch was a Caesar salad with chunks of chicken and a bottle of fizzy mineral water.

"You know," Holly said, "the scale of all this is weighing heavily on me."

"Get used to it," Stone replied. "It's not going to change."

"At State, I was always trying to save a buck here and there."

"The federal budget makes State's look like the widow's mite. Anyway, the cost of the airplane is spread over your transition, the Secret Service, and the Air Force, and maybe two or three other agencies we can't think of at the moment. And they all move on money. Fuel costs money. Airports cost money—that's why there are landing fees. It costs money to scrape the bugs off the windshield."

28

Stone and Holly were having breakfast in bed the following morning when Holly's phone rang. "Yes? Scrambled. Hi, there! What a good idea. I'll ask him." She turned toward Stone. "Kate wants you to come to D.C. with me and stay at the White House a few days, then we'll fly back."

Stone thought about it for a millisecond. "Okay."

"He's in. Yes, we'll be there for lunch. Bye-bye."

"Why does she want me there?" Stone asked.

"Because she enjoys your company. So does Will. Do you realize how few people she deals with daily whose company she does not enjoy?"

"I'd never thought about it."

"Now you know."

They arrived at Teterboro, and the airplane was on the ramp with the right engine already running. The car pulled up close, and Claire got out, unfolded the walker, and positioned it by the rear car door.

Stone got out, then turned to assist Holly. "Do this very slowly and very carefully, like you don't want to fall and break a hip." He helped her stand up and take a step to the walker. Claire was at her elbow. When they reached the airstairs, both Claire and Stone were right behind her, each taking an elbow, then the stewardess boarded with the walker and closed the door, and immediately the left engine started.

"Jesus," Holly said, struggling to get the coat off. "This thing weighs a ton!" She yanked off the wig. "And it's so hot!" She hung it on the walker and sat down, smoothing her hair, which was pinned up.

"Don't take the hair down," Claire said. "We don't have a hairdresser aboard to fix it when we arrive."

"Oh, all right," Holly said.

"I'm going to give you a little pep talk when we arrive," Claire said, "so you won't have to remember it any longer than it takes to get into the car."

Holly nodded, opened her briefcase, and started to read reports and documents.

Stone sat beside her, with Claire facing her. "You know," Claire said, "I think we can get a lot of mileage out of this wig and coat thing."

Holly rolled her eyes but said nothing.

Stone spoke up. "When that outfit wears out, you can strap her onto a stretcher and put her in an ambulance for the ride."

"Not without shooting me in the head first," Holly said, then went back to reading.

They set down at Manassas, Virginia, and before the airplane stopped rolling, a black Lincoln Town Car, maybe ten years old but impeccable, drove up to the left wingtip.

Claire helped Holly with the wig and the coat, and Stone preceded them down the airstairs, carrying the walker.

"All right, Grandma," he said, taking her elbow. "Cling to the walker, as if it were life itself, and don't forget to limp."

Holly performed beautifully, gripping the walker, while Stone supported her arm. He tucked her into the car and went around to the other door and got in. "Don't take off anything," he said. "You'll still need the disguise at the other end, so the White House staff won't recognize you."

"Harrumph!" Holly said.

"Lung cancer? That's good!"

The performance was repeated at the White House until they were safely in the elevator, and Holly started to shed things. She unpinned her hair and ran her fingers through it, looking remarkably put together.

In the family quarters they were shown to a suite at the opposite end of the apartment from where the Lees slept. Holly hung up her clothes, brushed her hair, and was ready. They walked down the hall to the living room and found President Katharine Lee already seated near the fireplace. Kisses and hugs were exchanged, and they sat down with glasses of iced tea.

A moment later, the vice president–elect, Senator Sam Meriwether, joined them. "Betsy sends her regrets," he said, referring to his wife. "She's got a walk-through of the Naval Observatory house with a decorator, and after that she'll have to select a couple of dozen paint colors and wallpapers and twice as many fabrics."

"We understand, Sam," Kate said.

Will Lee and their young son, Billy, arrived and shed their coats. "We just had a walk around the grounds," Will said.

The little boy gravely shook everyone's hand, then sat between his parents.

"Stone," Kate said. "How have you been spending your time?"

"Following Holly around, mostly," he replied.

"Get used to it," Will Lee said. "The pain goes away after a year or two."

"Swell," Stone said, "but I'll be spending most of my time in New York. I'll only get down here once in a while."

Holly leaned close and whispered, "Whenever I'm horny."

"Not that often," he whispered back.

After lunch, the Lees disappeared and Holly and Stone were left with Bill Wright and Claire Dunn.

"We're delighted with how well it went this morning," Bill said.

"Next time," Holly said, "I'll go as a mental patient, in a straitjacket."

"Too obvious," Stone said. "You're doing very well as my grandmother, which is how you were listed on the manifest."

"What do you hear from my pursuers?" Holly asked.

"We know they know you're coming to town, but they won't ever know you're in the White House . . . unless you make an unauthorized public appearance."

"I guess that rules out my favorite restaurants," Holly said.

"We can order for you and bring it here," Bill said.

"I'll hold you to that," Holly said. "There are few things I enjoy as much as dinner in a restaurant with friends."

"We can arrange for a few friends to be invited to dinners at the White House," Bill replied.

"Nobody ever turns down that invitation," Stone remarked.

"And then they can be surprised to find you here and be sworn to secrecy," Bill said.

"I'll give you a list," Holly said, "and I'll try to keep it short."

Claire suddenly produced a cell phone that had not rung. "Yes?" She listened some more. "Thank you." She hung up and turned to the others. "A maid at the Hay-Adams Hotel, across the street, found a sniper's rifle with a silencer attached, in a supply closet in the hotel.

As she spoke, other agents entered the room and closed the blinds on the Hay-Adams side of the White House.

"Does this mean I aged twenty years for nothing?" Holly asked.

29

Stone went over to the Hay-Adams with Bill Wright. They were walked to an upper-floor guest room by a Secret Service agent and found a suitcase lying on the bed, with a broken-down rifle fitted into it. A technician was dusting the room for fingerprints.

"Any prints on the weapon?" Stone asked.

"None," the tech replied. "Wiped clean. All we've found in here are the fingerprints of the maid."

"How is the silencer made?"

"A soft-drink can filled with sawdust. It might be effective on the first round, but not after that. Too insubstantial."

"Then the shooter is very confident of his skill," Stone said, looking out the window toward the White House across the street. "Anybody see him at check-in?"

The agent spoke up. "Tallish man in an overcoat and hat, paid cash in advance for one night. Used a false name. We've got nothing."

"I'm tired of having nothing," Bill said.

"How was the rifle discovered?"

"A maid found it when she removed a stack of towels from the closet."

"How did it get in here?"

"She called a bellman for help because the case was too heavy for her."

"Did the bellman show him to the room?"

"Yes. The man left a twenty-dollar tip. I guess the bellman was looking at the money, instead of his face. The man was of no help to us."

"You've got nothing," Stone said to Bill. Stone looked at his watch. "I'm late for lunch."

"I'll drive you over there," Bill said.

S tone walked in to find Holly, Sam Meriwether, and all three Lees at the table. "My apologies." He took a seat and started on his salad.

"Tell us about the gun."

"A Remington 700, a very popular hunting rifle. Serial number filed off, no prints."

"So you've got nothing?" Holly asked.

"That's exactly what we've got. It sounds worse when you say it."

"Have they done everything?"

"The police officer inside you would be satisfied."

"Did his room have a view of this room?"

"It did."

Bill Wright was invited in to give his report, which was identical to Stone's.

When he had gone, Kate said, "I invited him in so he wouldn't feel left out. Have you left anything out, Stone?"

"Only a suspicion."

"Let's hear it."

"It's all a little too simple. A man checks in with a suitcase, leaves it in a closet, where it would surely be found in due course, then leaves. He couldn't have hit Holly through that window unless she was deliberately standing close to it."

"Why would I do that?" Holly asked.

"My very point."

"Why would they make a plan for nothing?" Kate asked.

"Because they have another plan, and they want

the police to believe they've been thwarted. They may also have wanted to send the Secret Service a message that they can't be easily shaken off."

"Did you share your theories with Bill?"

"Yes, on the way back here."

"What was his reaction?"

"A sort of grunt."

"Did you think he came to the same conclusion?"

"I doubt it. Bill was not trained as a crime solver; that isn't the Secret Service's mission."

"What did the police think?"

"No policemen were there. I'm not sure if they had been called yet. Hotel security would have known to call the Secret Service. That done, they may not have bothered with the police, they'd think the Secret Service would involve them."

"Any press?"

"I doubt if hotel security would call them. It isn't the sort of publicity they seek."

Kate changed the subject, and no one resisted.

After lunch, Kate took Holly into her study and retrieved some notes from her desk drawer. "Now that you're the president-elect, there are some things I can share with you that might be of assistance after you've taken the oath."

"I'd be grateful for any advice," Holly said.

"You may be sorry you said that," Kate replied.
She pulled a fat briefcase from under her desk and
handed it across. "These are files on every congressman and senator: short bio, legislative record,
photos of him or her and spouse, peccadillos. If
you can commit them to memory, you'll impress
the hell out of everybody."

"Thank you, I'll try."

Kate took her through every position, foreign
and domestic, that her administration held,
discussed the work of the intelligence services at
length, talked about the military hierarchy, and
supplied the same information about them that
she had about Congress.

Kate then placed two fat volumes on her desk.
"Here's a digest of the most recent national
budget we've passed. By the way, everything I'm
giving you will also be available on your computer; you'll be issued the latest in desktops and
laptops, all with encryption."

Another thick book described the nation's
nuclear arsenal and its capabilities. "This should
not leave the White House," Kate said.

"I've already sent your transition team a list of
the White House staff, along with recommendations for which ones you should retain, if you can.

A lot of them will want to go make some money. Eight or even four years is a long time for a family to live on a White House salary."

"I can understand that," Holly said. "State Department salaries are no better."

"I've set up the room next to this one as a temporary study for you, and I've assigned you a very knowledgeable assistant, starting tomorrow morning. She'll help you with the computer system, especially, and she knows everybody here and on the Hill quite well. Her name is Barbara Tanner. She's the sort of person you'll want to keep on, so be nice to her."

They spent another two hours at all this, and Holly went back to her room for a nap before drinks, feeling a little weighed down with information.

30

Sykes sat at his dining table and surveyed his people. "Where's Bess?" one of them asked. "Good question. Not here yet."

"That's troubling."

Bess strode in from the living room. "Don't be troubled. Traffic accident on the road, that's all." She pulled up a chair.

"Good," Sykes said. "How'd it go?"

"As planned," somebody said. "As far as we can tell, they bought it, hook, line, and sinker. They'll be wasting a lot of manpower guarding the hotel."

"Where's Eugene?" Sykes asked.

"Holed up at the apartment you rented. He's moved in."

"Good. We want him to be seen around the building and the neighborhood, to become a part of the wallpaper, so to speak."

"He moved in with two suitcases of clothes that he's worn once or twice."

"Good. When he leaves we don't want it to look like he's fled the scene. We've sent him a couple of boxes of books and some little stuff to make it look like he's staying awhile. Has he slept there yet?"

"Tonight's his first night."

"She's not going to stay there forever," Sykes said.

"We've caught sight of her working at a desk for periods of time. It's a better shot from the roof than the hotel window."

Bess was taking all this in, but not asking any questions. If Sykes felt she needed to know something, he'd tell her. She knew him well enough by now to know that.

"Here's how it's going to go," Sykes said. "Eugene will carry in his case holding the rifle and the new silencer; he'll do that this afternoon. He will wear cotton gloves the whole time he's in the apartment. Before sunup tomorrow he will go to the roof and build himself a little nest in a corner, just enough to hide his presence. Once that's up, he'll get the rifle assembled and on its tripod. Then he will wait until she appears at the desk and fire four shots. Pulling the trigger once fires twice—the first two shots will weaken and penetrate the window and the second pull will kill with two head shots. Nobody in the building or the neighborhood will hear anything. The new silencer has been tested; it's excellent, if I do say so.

"After the kill, he will take the rifle apart, pack it in the case, then take it down a floor to the rear fire escape and drop it from the top level into the garden, where it will be collected and taken away by Arnie. Then Eugene will return to his apartment. He will be dressed in pajamas and a robe and will make himself breakfast and leave the dishes in the sink. He will sit down and read the **Washington Post** until the first searchers arrive; he will greet them at the door with the newspaper in hand and let them have a look around and answer their questions. He will be curious about their reasons for calling, but they will tell him nothing. He will show them the Maryland driver's license we furnished him with and the passport made by the same craftsman. They'll leave him to his newspaper and go.

"Eugene will stay there for another day or two before walking away with nothing but his brief-case. We've paid two months' rent and a security deposit, so the apartment won't be looked at again until he fails to pay the rent. By that time, every-body will have forgotten about him. He won't have a beard anymore, and that will help. There won't be any of his fingerprints to be found, and not so much as a hair on the shoulder of a jacket. He will, in short, be untraceable.

"Also, no one here at this moment will leave this house until after Eugene checks out of his building, and I want all your cell phones on the table now."

Bess unhesitatingly laid hers on the table, and it was collected with everyone else's. "Have you provided any entertainment for us, Colonel?" she asked, getting a chuckle from the others.

"Yes, there's the TV, and you may have the run of my library. Did you bring a suitcase, as directed?"

"Yes, it's in the car."

"Go and get it, then. Your room is the first on the right at the top of the stairs. You may as well put your things away."

"Of course." She got up, left the house, went to her car, and popped the trunk. She set her suitcase on the ground, then opened a side panel and extracted a burner phone and a .380 semi-automatic pistol, tucking the phone into a pocket of her jeans and the pistol into an ankle holster. Then she closed the trunk, walked back to the house, and started up the stairs.

"Just a minute," a male voice said. She turned to find one of her companions, whose name was Earl, standing there. "Colonel's orders: I'm to have a look in your suitcase."

She handed the case over the rail and stood on the stairs while he placed it on a table, opened it, and searched it thoroughly. He closed it and returned it to her. "Thanks."

"Anytime," she said, and continued to her room. Once inside, she duct-taped the pistol to the bottom of a desk drawer and retrieved her burner phone, sat down on the bed, and turned it on. It took a moment to boot up.

"Shit!" she said aloud. "No bars." There was no cell service in this room; she'd have to try others. She tucked the instrument into her pocket, put away her clothes, then walked downstairs. The house was empty except for Elroy, who was working in the kitchen. She got a look at the phone in each room, and there were no bars showing in any of them.

She went back to the kitchen. "Where is everybody, Elroy?" she asked.

"They left with the colonel," Elroy said. "Maybe gone to D.C."

"All of them?"

"All the ones here at breakfast. I don't know who's in the bunkhouse."

She left the house through the kitchen door and walked through the breezeway to the bunkhouse, which was empty, then she went back to the kitchen. "Elroy," she said, "I'm going to take a little hike up the hill over there." She jerked a thumb toward the hill where Eugene had been practicing his marksmanship. "Anybody asks, that's where I can be found."

"Okay," Elroy said.

"Can you make me a sandwich, please?"

"Sure," Elroy said, and began busying himself making and toasting the sandwich.

Bess pulled up a chair to the kitchen table. "I hear you're an ex-Navy man," she said.

"That's right," he replied.

"Is that where you learned to cook?"

"Nope. I learned to cook at my mama's knee. I only cook Southern. That was all she taught me, but I don't seem to get any complaints."

"Certainly not from me," Bess said. She accepted the sandwich in a brown paper bag, and

Elroy opened the refrigerator door to display beer and soft drinks. She selected a diet soda and dropped it into the bag. "Thanks, Elroy, I owe you one," she said.

"Think nothing of it," he said, then went back to rolling biscuits.

Bess left by the back door and set a good pace for herself, following a well-worn footpath.

31

The path was steep, and Bess judged the top of the hill to be somewhere between 100 and 150 feet above the level where the compound was located.

At the top, she sat on a boulder and panted until her breathing returned to normal, then, with trepidation, she got out the cell phone. What if there was no reception up here? She turned it on and got two bars, sometimes one, sometimes none. Dicey.

She direct-dialed Tom Blake's cell phone.

"Blake."

"It's me. Can you record this? It's important."

"Just a minute." There were sounds of fumbling, then the line went dead.

She redialed.

"Blake."

"I've got a weak signal here, so I may have to repeat myself to get it all recorded."

"It's recording now."

"The man in charge has rented an apartment on the same side of the big house. The shooter will establish a firing position on the roof of that building. They're planning the shoot for tomorrow morning when the subject often works at a desk. Got that?"

"Repeat it, just in case."

She did so. "To continue, the weapon fires two rounds with each pull of the trigger. He will wait until the subject settles at the desk, then fire once to break or weaken the window, then once more.

"The shooter will drop his case off the back of the building, into a garden, where it will be immediately recovered and removed. He will go back to his apartment, dress in pajamas and a robe, where he will be found by searchers, reading the morning papers. He will not leave the building for a couple of days, then he'll walk away with only a briefcase and not return. Rent is paid for two months. Got all that?"

"Hang on while I replay." The line went dead again, and when she redialed, the signal was weaker, and the call didn't go through. She continued to try for a couple of minutes, then stopped, not wanting to run down the battery.

She ate her sandwich and enjoyed the sun for an hour, then tried the call again. No good. She looked up and, in the distance, saw dust rising from a car on the dirt road approaching the compound. She paced off ten feet, then hid the burner phone under a rock and went back to her seat on the boulder. The car pulled into the parking area at the compound, and the colonel got out. He seemed to be looking at her, so she waved and got a wave back. He beckoned to her, and she started down the trail.

The colonel was at his desk in his study when she entered. "You wanted me?"

"What were you doing on the hilltop?" he asked.

"Enjoying the view. It's quite a climb up there."

"Yes, it is. Do you have a cell phone, other than the one you turned in?"

"No," she said.

"Grab the desk and spread 'em," he said.

She assumed the position and tried to be patient while he patted down every inch of her, spending extra time at her breasts and crotch.

"Well, there's no cell reception out here, anyway," he said. "Except at the hilltop."

"I wouldn't know about that," she said.

He opened a desk drawer. "Which phone is yours?"

"The white iPhone," she replied, and he handed it to her.

"There's no Wi-Fi here, unless I turn it on, which I do a couple of times a day to check e-mail."

"Mostly, I get spam anyway," she said, tucking the phone in a pocket.

"Don't we all?"

"If you'll excuse me, I'm going to go take a nap," she said.

"No lunch?"

"Elroy made me a sandwich for my hike."

"See you at dinner then."

She went back to her room and turned on her iPhone. She found an e-mail from a box with her dead father's name on it.

> Mom got your card, but she complained about not being able to read your handwriting. Next time, print block letters.
>
> Love, Dad

Bill Wright and Tom Blake sat in an empty cubicle in the Secret Service's small office space, on a lower level in the White House.

Tom replayed his recording from Elizabeth.

"Jesus, that's terrible," Bill said. "Is that all you got?"

"I've got some tech people working to see if they can improve it," Tom said, "but I'm doubtful. If it had been an e-mail, we might have a shot at putting it together, but I don't see how they could do that with a voice message."

"Well, I heard something about an apartment and a roof and a garden," Bill said.

"Yeah, I got that, too. Maybe they're going to shoot from a rooftop?"

Bill went to a cabinet and got out a large, rolled-up sheet of paper. "What if, as we suspected, the rifle at the Hay-Adams was a kind of decoy, designed to waste our time?" He unrolled the paper and pinned it to a message board in the office. It was a satellite shot of the White House and the surrounding area. He pinned a sheet of clear plastic over it and found a grease pencil. "Here's the Hay-Adams," he said, drawing a circle around it. "But I don't see an apartment building in either direction from it."

"No, there's the Chamber of Commerce building and a lot of courts and other government buildings," Tom replied, "but there's no building that would house apartments."

"This just doesn't make any sense," Bill said. "God, I wish she'd had better cell service."

"Maybe we'd do better looking out the window we were worried about," Tom said.

Bill picked up a phone. "This is Agent Wright. Are the family quarters occupied at the moment?" He listened. "Please ring up there and say that Assistant Director Blake of the FBI and I are coming up, and let the agent on duty know, too." He unpinned the map and rolled it up. "Come on," he said.

The two men walked up to the main floor of the White House and found the elevator to the family quarters. They walked out of the elevator into a broad hallway with a seating area at one end. A Secret Service agent stood at the front door of the quarters.

The agent was unknown to Bill, so both men handed him their identification before being admitted to the quarters. "Is the president in the residence?" Bill asked the agent.

"No, sir. She's making a speech somewhere. There's just the president-elect and a Mr. Barrington. Last time I checked she was in her temporary office, next to the president's study."

"Right," Bill said. "This way, Tom."

32

Bill Wright rapped on the door.

"Come in!" A woman's voice.

He opened the door. Holly Barker was sitting at a large desk, its top obscured by stacks of bound documents.

"What can I do for you, Bill?" she asked.

"Ma'am, this is Tom Blake, assistant director of the FBI for criminal investigations."

"Hello, Tom."

"Hello, ma'am."

"We'd like to take a look outside your window," Bill said.

"Help yourself. Am I in the way?"

"I'll let you know in a minute."

The two men went and stood by the window, which was made of a thick plate glass. And between two layers, a fine wire mesh could be detected.

Tom rapped on the window with his class ring, which, he reflected, was about all it was good for. "Is this going to stop a bullet?" he asked.

"We believe so," Bill said, "but it was installed before my time, so I haven't seen any test results."

"A high-powered rifle's bullet?" Tom asked.

"Same answer."

"Ma'am," Tom said. "May I sit in your chair for a moment?"

Holly rose and stepped aside.

Bill unrolled the satshot and oriented it properly. "Okay," he said. "There would be the possibility of a hit from anyplace we can see out the window." He marked the limits on the satshot.

"Everything I can see from here," Tom said, "with two exceptions, looks like government to me."

Bill looked out the window and compared it with the map. "I agree. The two exceptions are the Hay-Adams Hotel and an Episcopal church." He pointed to both on the map.

Tom checked the view again, then returned to the map. "What's this building next to the church?"

"The rectory, I think."

"I'm a Baptist. What happens in a rectory?"

"Church offices, maybe a residence or two."

"There's a row of identical windows along the top floor that could be individual rooms or small apartments," Tom said.

"Maybe for staff or priests or other employees."

"What's behind the rectory?"

Bill checked and tapped the satshot with a finger. "A garden."

"What we can hear on the tape is about an apartment where they've paid two months' rent."

"Agreed."

"And we agree that there are no other residential buildings within rifle range of that window except for the rectory?"

"We do."

"Then let's go take a look at it," Tom said.

"We're sorry to have disturbed you, ma'am," Bill said. "Would you mind if we relocate your desk? It's for your personal safety."

"Anywhere you like."

"On the other side of the building would be nice," Tom muttered.

"Not possible," Bill said. "Give me a hand with this."

"Where is it going?"

"All the way over there in that corner. I'm afraid, ma'am, that won't leave you with much of a view."

"Nor for the shooter," Holly replied. "I like it."

The desk, with its load of documents was very heavy, but they eventually managed to slide it across the carpet and into position.

"There," Bill said.

Holly pushed her chair over to the desk and sat down. "I can't see a thing outside the window."

"Good," Tom said.

"Tom," Bill said. "Does the FBI have some sort of a department that could put a dummy in a chair near the window?"

"Yes. It's called the Department of Special Services."

"Make her a tall redhead," Bill said.

Tom got out his phone. "No service," he said.

"That's because of the wire mesh in the plate glass."

"You can use a house phone in the living room," Holly said. "The White House operator can connect you with any phone in the world."

"That'll do," Tom said, and they left her alone, closing the door behind them.

Tom picked up a phone on a sofa-side table and made his call.

———

The two men sat in the office of the bishop, who was regarding them askance. "You want to search the rectory?"

"That is correct, sir. It's a matter of safety for the White House."

The bishop looked at the two IDs on his desk. "Who are you looking for?"

"A man with a high-powered rifle, but he won't have arrived yet."

"I'm glad to hear it." He spoke to his assistant. "Eric, please find the keys to the rooms on the upper floors of the rectory and escort these gentlemen there for a tour. Make sure they don't steal the silver." He handed back the IDs. "Good luck to you."

What's on the upper floors?" Bill asked Eric as the elevator rose.

"Top floor is sort of a dormitory that used to house visiting high-school kids who did summer internships. It isn't used anymore. There are a few single rooms, as well, for their teachers. One floor down is busy office space."

"Let's see the top floor," Bill said.

As they got out of the elevator a maid stepped out of a door, towing a mop bucket behind her.

"Miss, which rooms did you clean?" Tom asked.

"All of the singles. We do it once a week, though they're little used."

"Are they locked?" Eric asked.

"No, sir."

"There are three furnished," Eric said. "Which do you want to see?"

"All of them," Tom replied

The three were identically furnished with a bed, a desk, a padded chair, and two lamps. There were fresh towels in the bathrooms.

"Which of the rear windows in the dormitory have views of the garden?" Bill asked.

"I suppose the ones across from these rooms."

Tom tried the windows in all three rooms. Only one opened freely. The others were nailed shut.

"There used to be an air conditioner in that window," Eric said, "before the whole place got new ductwork."

Bill walked across the dormitory and found one window that would open. "Nice view of the garden," he said when he returned.

"I noticed locks on the doors of the three rooms," Tom said. "Where are the keys?"

Eric held up a bunch of, perhaps two dozen keys. "Help yourself."

"Okay," Tom said, "let's lock the rooms on either side. We can put men in both. He'll have only one option and one working window."

"I'd call that boxing him in," Bill said.

33

Bill Wright and Tom Blake sat in Holly's temporary office and watched as two FBI technicians worked. They set up a card table in front of the window and placed the dummy, dressed in a white blouse and a red wig, in a chair between the window and the table. They borrowed several thick documents from Holly's desk and arranged them on the card table, then placed the dummy's left hand on an open document and her right hand, holding a pencil, on another document. They set a lamp on the table and plugged it into a receptacle under the window.

"Would you turn on that light switch, please,

Mr. Blake?" the tech in charge asked, pointing to a switch beside the door. Bill did so, and the light came on. Also, the head of the dummy, which had been pointed down at the open document, turned to its right, and its right hand made small movements, as if writing.

"Wonderful!" Bill said "From a distance it will be indistinguishable from the lady herself."

"I agree," Tom said. "Thank you, gentlemen."

The two techs closed their tool kits and prepared to depart.

"How will we turn it on tomorrow morning?" Tom asked.

"We're not going to have access at dawn," Bill replied.

"Why don't you just leave the light switch on?" the lead tech said. "It's a fresh lightbulb; it won't burn out overnight."

"Good idea," Bill said

The two men took their tools and left. Wright and Blake departed with them, leaving the light switch on.

The dummy continued doing its work.

At three AM, they circled the block, checking for police, then stopped at the gate to the church gardens. "Can you handle the lock?" the driver asked Eugene.

"I can handle just about any lock," Eugene replied. "Honk, if you spot a cop." He got out of the car, took his case, and walked to the gate, perhaps thirty feet away. He removed an instrument that looked like a small electric drill from his case, inserted one end in the lock, and opened it in under twenty seconds. He closed his case and let himself into the garden, then applied a piece of duct tape to the lock's bolt, so that it wouldn't lock him in. That done, he walked up the stone path to the rear of the rectory and unlocked the rear door by the same means.

Inside, he made sure he could open it without a key, then walked to the elevator and took it to the top floor. He was surprised to find two of the single rooms locked, but the third one was not. He pulled on a pair of soft, thin leather gloves and let himself into the room, then set his case on the bed and opened it.

The case contained the dismantled rifle, scope, and silencer; his lock pick; and a coil of nylon rope with a half-hook at one end, the whole length tied in a series of knots. He walked across the dormitory room, opened the unlocked window, laid the half-hook over the sill and tossed the rope out into the night air. He watched to see that the other end nearly touched the ground.

He returned to the room, locked the door behind him, and then practiced assembling and disassembling the rifle as quickly as possible, something he had rehearsed many times in his room. He set up the folding tripod, attached the rifle, and sighted across the avenue to the White House, where a single window of the family quarters was lit. To his astonishment, the woman was sitting at a desk, going through a document and making notes.

"Good God, an insomniac," he said.

He checked his equipment again, then it occurred to him: Why wait? His chances of pulling this off and getting away were better now than in the morning. He got out his cell phone and speed-dialed a number.

"Yes?"

"Conditions are favorable at this hour," he said.

"**Now?**" came the astonished reply.

"I repeat: conditions are favorable now. Plans change. Position the vehicle."

"As you wish."

"How long do you need?"

"Three minutes."

"Ring once when you're in position."

"Understood."

Both men hung up.

Eugene made his final preparations, then sighted through the rifle again. She was still at work. He positioned himself behind the rifle, took aim, and waited.

The cell phone in his breast pocket vibrated once. Eugene squeezed off the first shot. He saw the window star; it would be much weakened now. He squeezed off the second shot, saw the window explode and the woman's hair move. Then he saw a red flashing light under the eaves near the window and heard a bell start to ring rhythmically. The shattering of the window had tripped an alarm system. He wasn't going to bother with changing into pajamas; he had to get out **now**.

Quickly and smoothly, he closed the window, disassembled the rifle, packing each piece into its place, closed the case, unlocked the door and walked quickly to the open window in the dorm. He looked out the window, chose a thicket of bushes, and dropped the case. He saw it disappear into the shrubs.

He straddled the windowsill, checked that the half-hook was holding, then climbed out the window and slid down the rope, controlling his descent with the knots. Once on the ground, he flicked the rope twice; the half-hook popped off the windowsill and fell to the ground. He retrieved his case from the bushes, tucked the rope inside it, and ran for the gate, removing the duct tape as he left. The car was waiting.

Eugene tossed his case into the rear compartment of the SUV. "No more than thirty miles an hour," he said. The driver pulled away and drove, unobserved, through the empty streets.

At three AM, Bill Wright was dressed and having toast and coffee in his kitchen. He and Blake were meeting at the rectory at four AM. His phone rang. "Wright," he said.

"Code 101 at location zero," a voice said.

Wright was stunned. "What damage?"

"To be determined."

Wright put away his phone and ran for his car. The second call came as he was backing out of his garage.

"It's Tom. Did you hear?"

"I'm on my way. I'll meet you there." He hung up and switched on his flashing lights.

The White House gate guard waved him through quickly. He drove to the portico, got out, and ran for the elevator.

CHOPPY WATER

Tom Blake was already in the room, along with two uniformed Secret Service guards. Holly Barker and the president and the first gentleman were also in the room, all of them dressed in nightclothes and robes.

Bill said good evening to them, then walked to the window and inspected it. There was a hole the size of a softball in the two layers of glass. "Upgrade needed here," he said to nobody in particular.

He bent over and inspected the dummy. "Two shots to the head."

"Then I must be deceased," Holly said.

34

Colonel Sykes was sound asleep when he was awakened by the telephone. The bedside clock read 3:33 AM, and the shoot was to take place after seven AM. Something had gone wrong. "Hello?"

"Confirm project has been successfully completed," Eugene's voice said.

"You must be confused," Sykes said. "Too early."

"Subject is an insomniac. Favorable conditions prevailed earlier than planned." He hung up.

Sykes sat on his bed, his heart pounding. He had made it happen, just as he had planned, only sooner. He looked up the number of Eugene's burner phone and dialed it.

"Yes?"

"Confirm successful completion."

"Confirmed. It was perfect."

"Listen to me: don't arrive carrying the package. Leave it where you can find it again. Also, any relevant clothing. Do not make your final turn if there is any vehicle in sight."

"Understood," Eugene said, then hung up.

Sykes breathed a sigh of relief and began to calm down. They would get rid of the rifle and tools and not lead anyone to the compound. All that remained was to get his people to bed, and it would be over.

There was a knock at his door. "Wade?" Bess was awake.

"Come in."

She opened the door and stepped inside, wearing a robe. "I was awakened by voices. Is everything all right?"

"It was just a phone call," he said. "Everything is all right. Go back to bed."

"You sounded very tense," she said.

"How could you hear me from across the hall?"

"You tend to shout when you're tense," she said.

"You're right, I do. Now please go back to bed and don't come out until breakfast time."

"All right." She shut the door, and he heard her door close.

She turned on her iPhone and checked it: no phone service, no Wi-Fi, no e-mails received. She lay back down and tried to sleep, but could only rest. Finally, as dawn broke, she got up, showered, washed and dried her hair, and dressed. She walked into the dining room at seven sharp. No one was there.

She heard men laughing outside and peeked out a window. Sykes, Eugene, and the other man were obviously elated. She left the dining room and didn't return until she heard them come in. "Good morning," she said cheerfully.

"Good morning," the three of them said together.

"You're looking very pleased with yourself," she said to Sykes. "Has something good happened?"

"I don't know," Sykes replied, reaching for a TV remote control. "Let's check CNN."

A woman was standing on the White House lawn, microphone in her hand. "This is the statement issued a few minutes ago," she said. "'Last night, very late, a breach of White House security occurred. A member of the staff was injured, is being treated at a local hospital, and is expected to recover.' That's all we have at the moment."

"No name or gender of the person injured?" the anchorperson asked.

"No, just what I read. Everyone is very tight-lipped, as you might expect when a member of the White House staff has been injured."

The anchorperson turned to other stories, and Sykes switched off the TV.

"'Injured'?" Eugene asked, clearly surprised.

Sykes cut him off with a sharp glance. "That's what she said. We'll hear more later."

They continued their breakfast in silence. "I have to get to work," Bess said. "Will you excuse me?"

"Of course," Sykes replied. "Will we see you at the weekend?"

"If you like."

"I like."

She left, gathered up her purse and her coat, got into her car, and departed.

Sykes stood up. "Eugene," he said. "I want you to go up to the top of the hill, to the spot where you were shooting the other day, and see if you can find a cell phone."

"What would a cell phone be doing up there?" Eugene asked. "You've got all the phones."

"Look for a burner," he said, "and be thorough. Work your way outward from where you were firing."

Bill Wright and Tom Blake sat at a table in the White House mess with George Perkins, the head of the White House Secret Service detail.

"My people have been over the rectory with a fine-tooth comb," Perkins said. "Nothing was disturbed, no new fingerprints found, no gunshot residue detected. The only thing that might have been out of place was an open window overlooking the garden, and they think a maid might have done that yesterday when it got warm upstairs. The cleaning staff will be questioned as soon as they arrive at work."

Bill Wright spoke up. "I think we need to get the president-elect out of here today. I've already called Barrington on my own authority, and his airplane will arrive around eleven AM, at Manassas."

"You didn't run that by your director?" Tom asked.

"No. I'm in charge of her personal detail until she's sworn in on January 20."

"What did your director have to say about what happened?"

"I haven't spoken to him yet, and I won't until we're in the air."

"I didn't hear that," George Perkins said.

"Don't worry, George, I'll take whatever heat there may be."

"I don't see how you could be in any trouble," Tom said. "After all, we prevented an assassination." His phone rang, and he checked the incoming number before stepping away from the table. "Yes?"

"It's me," Elizabeth said. "What the hell happened at the White House early this morning?"

"There was an attempt on her life, but the shooter hit a dummy we had set up. Everyone here is fine."

"No one in the hospital?"

"That was a cover story."

"I was awakened by Sykes's telephone last night. He's across the hall from my room."

"What time did the call come in?"

"A little after three-thirty."

"His man was reporting in," Tom said.

"They were outside talking when I came down for breakfast. They were excited and elated."

"Eugene reported a successful hit, and it was, but on the dummy."

"I got your e-mail," she said. "I take it my message wasn't received."

"It was very broken, but it got us looking. The shot was fired from the rectory at the Episcopal church across the way from the White House. Wright and I checked it out yesterday, and we had planned to be there at four AM, but they turned up early and were long gone when we got there."

"I heard the White House report on TV."

"That was about making them think they had succeeded."

"Well, it worked. Now what?"

"Did anything happen at Sykes's compound that would stand up as evidence for an arrest?"

"Just what I told you."

"When are you going back out there?"

"This weekend."

"Sykes clearly doesn't trust you."

"That's because I'm not sleeping with him. I told him I'm a lesbian."

"And he wouldn't trust a lesbian?"

"Not in a century. But I wasn't willing to fuck him to gain his trust. I'm a lousy undercover agent, right?"

"I like you better lousy. Keep me posted over the weekend."

"It's not easy. There's no cell service, and Wi-Fi is only turned on a couple of times a day, to receive messages."

"Do the best you can." They both hung up.

35

Stone and Holly were having breakfast when Bill Wright came into the residence. "You folks ready?"

"As soon as we've finished breakfast," Holly said.

"The Lincoln is waiting for you. I'll get your luggage. Don't forget your disguise. And the walker."

Holly sighed. "You haven't convinced me about the disguise. After all, they found me."

"They found a dummy, ma'am. They don't know where you are."

They took off shortly after eleven. Bill came and sat down with them. "I want to bring you up to date."

"Thank you," Holly said. "I'd like that."

"We think we know who did this, but we can't prove it, I'm sorry to say. We have a mole in their camp, but they don't trust her enough to tell her these things in advance."

"It's a woman?" Stone asked.

"It is. She's an FBI agent who's been assigned to the Justice Department for several weeks. There's no cell service at the colonel's compound, but she managed to get a garbled message out about the attack."

"And who are the group?"

"The top man is a retired Army colonel named Wade Sykes."

"I've heard that name before," Holly said. "He left under some sort of cloud, didn't he?"

"Yes. He was charged with distributing white-supremacy materials on several Army bases, but he agreed to resign if they didn't prosecute him. He's quite well connected in Washington, especially among the right-wingers in Congress."

"Will he keep trying?" Stone asked.

"I will be surprised if he doesn't," Bill replied. "Pretty soon he'll find out that his attempt failed, and I expect that will humiliate him."

"I think you'd better stay at my house," Stone said.

"No," Holly replied. "I'm not going to run from this bastard."

"We're working with the FBI on this," Bill said, "and they're going to set up surveillance on Sykes's compound. If he or anyone else leaves the place, he'll be followed. I'm working with Tom Blake, the assistant director, and he's setting up the surveillance. He'll also have some people on the street for you."

They began the descent into Teterboro, and Bill went back to his seat.

They met at a restaurant in Georgetown. "When are you going back out there?" Tom asked Elizabeth.

"Tomorrow," she said.

"Has he asked you to be there at that time?"

"No, he just asked if I'd be back for the weekend, and I said I would, if he wanted me to be. We didn't mention a time."

"How many vehicles live at the place?"

"Sykes drives a silver Ford Explorer, pretty new. There's a van, and Eugene seems to drive that more than anyone else. The cook, Elroy Hubbard, drives a Toyota station wagon, but I don't think he's really a part of the group. Sykes won't talk about anything when he's in the room."

"All right," Bill said, placing a leatherette pouch on the table. "There are two trackers in this package. I want you to place them on Sykes's Explorer and the van."

"All right."

"They have lithium ion batteries and only operate when they detect movement. Don't place them in the wheel wells; they're too easy to find there. Wait until dark, then crawl under each vehicle and place the trackers where they can't be seen by just bending over and looking underneath. Somewhere around the gas tank might work; it's up to you. They're marked number one and two, and there is an on-off switch on each. So turn them on; they'll stay dark until there's movement."

"All right."

"Do you still have your burner phone?"

"I hid it on the hilltop when I tried to call you from there."

"Here's another one," Tom said, handing it to her.

"Okay. Sykes turns on his Wi-Fi a couple of times a day, so if you send me a message, I'll get it eventually. I like the way you did it the last one; keep being Dad."

"If there's an emergency, I'll use the word 'may' in a message, meaning 'mayday.' If you get one like that, get out, and do whatever you have to do to protect yourself. You still have a gun?"

"Yes."

"If you have to think about whether to shoot somebody, shoot him. Thinking time is dangerous. If somebody is a threat, shoot him in the head. You don't want him to get up and start shooting at you."

"I wasn't trained to shoot people in the head," she said.

"It's just common sense. You're still using the .380, aren't you?"

"Yes."

"It doesn't carry the kind of punch that a .40 or .45 caliber would, so if you have to shoot, shoot to kill."

She nodded, but she didn't mean it.

Eugene left the table, got into the van, and went to retrieve his rifle case, which was hidden at a rest stop a mile or so from the turnoff to the compound. He took it back to his room, assembled the rifle, and slung it over his shoulder. "I'm going to do a little shooting," he said to his roommate.

Eugene went outside and began the climb to his perch on the hilltop. After resting for a couple of minutes, he set down the rifle and began his search for a cell phone. He walked in a circle around the hilltop, widening his path on each circuit, kicking at rocks and other debris as he went, looking into nooks and crannies. He sat down on a boulder and rested again before walking back down the path.

As he got up, he noticed that the boulder was loose. He pushed it over with a foot, and there, dug into the dirt, was a cheap cell phone. Sykes would be pleased.

36

Bess was driving down to Virginia when she passed a liquor store and remembered that Sykes's bar was out of Knob Creek. They had all been drinking it. She parked, went inside, and bought three bottles of the bourbon.

At the compound she took her suitcase in one hand and the shopping bag from the liquor store in the other and went inside. She left her suitcase on the stairs, then knocked on the door of Sykes's study. No answer. She knocked again, then went in and left a bottle of Knob Creek on the butler's tray that he used for a bar, then took the other two into the dining room and put them with the rest of the booze.

"That's very generous of you," a voice said from behind her. She turned and saw Sykes standing in the doorway.

"Well," she said. "I've been drinking a lot of it, so I thought I'd return some to the fold."

"Thank you. I'm sure we'll all appreciate it." He beckoned her into the study. "Sit down."

"I put a bottle with your stock, too," she said, nodding at the butler's tray. Then she sat down. "What's up?"

He set her burner phone on the table between them. "What's this?"

She picked it up, opened it, tried to turn it on, and failed. "It's a throwaway cell phone," she said. "The old-fashioned kind, not a smartphone. Dead."

"We found it at the top of the hill, where Eugene does his target practice."

"And . . . ?"

"And, I wondered if it was yours," he said, his gaze steady.

"No, mine is an iPhone, remember?"

"Maybe we should charge the throwaway."

"I don't have a charger for something that old, just for my iPhone."

"Well, I couldn't find one in your room. Everybody else has denied ownership of the throwaway. That leaves you."

"No," she said. "More likely it leaves one of them who's lying. The phone is not mine."

"You mind if we fingerprint you and make comparisons?"

"Go right ahead. You fingerprinted me when I first came here, remember? All you need is a print from the phone." She was sure she had wiped it down, and she hoped she had done so thoroughly.

"Only Eugene's prints are on it," Sykes said.

"Perhaps Eugene found his own phone," she said.

"Why do you say that?" he asked.

"Because you know it's not yours. I know it's not mine. And Eugene's prints are on it. Were his the only ones?"

"There was one other," Sykes said. "It doesn't match anyone here. We're running it through the national register."

"Wow! How do you get access to that?"

"We have friends everywhere."

"You certainly do. What will you do if the odd print belongs to one of the other men?"

"Take him out and shoot him, I suppose."

"Well, that's decisive."

"I'm a decisive man; when I find that I've been betrayed, I act decisively."

"I admire that in a man."

"I thought you preferred women."

"I prefer decisiveness in men. I prefer fucking women."

"Is that what, ah, you girls call it?"

"We look at fucking as an act of sex in general, not one in particular."

"I read that in a novel once," Sykes said.

"Perhaps we read the same fiction."

"I doubt it."

"I doubt it, too."

Sykes stood up. "Thanks for the bourbon," he said, then left the room.

Bess thought about which of the men she had seen on the hilltop. Just two: Eugene and his friend Earl. Then she had a thought. She went into the kitchen where Elroy was making biscuits. "I'm a little peckish, Elroy," she said. "May I have a biscuit?"

Elroy flipped one from a hot pan onto a saucer, opened it with his knife, and buttered it. "There you go," he said, handing her the saucer.

She bit into it and burned her tongue a little. "Fresh from the oven," she said, fanning her mouth.

"Sorry about that," Elroy said. "They're best hot."

She blew on the biscuit and attempted another bite. "Better," she said.

"Always."

"Elroy, may I ask you a question?"

"As long as you don't expect an honest answer," he replied.

"It's not all that personal. Have you ever been to the top of the hill out there?" She pointed her chin at the outside.

"Sure. I go up there and set a spell now and then."

"Have you ever taken a cell phone up there?"

Elroy looked at her appraisingly. "Why do you ask?"

"Because Eugene found one up there, and Sykes is pissed off about it. He says he found a fingerprint on it that isn't Eugene's or the rest of his guys' or mine. He also says that if he finds out who it is, he's going to take him out and shoot him."

Elroy looked at her curiously, but didn't reply immediately. "Do you think he would do that?" he asked, finally.

"I think he might. You must know that there's something going on around here."

"Generally," he said, "I keep my ass in the kitchen."

"A wise decision. I just wanted you to know, just in case it's your print."

Now he looked at her more curiously. "Who do you work for?" he asked.

"I work for a guy at the Justice Department. What about you?"

"I'm self-employed," Elroy replied. "I do contract work for Sykes."

"Fine by me," she said.

"Thanks for thinking of me," he replied, then went back to making biscuits.

Bess took her biscuit off the saucer and put that in the sink, then she walked outside, munching. She was safe, she was sure about that. She wasn't sure about Elroy.

Elroy was taking his biscuits out of the oven when Sykes walked into the room.

"Got a minute, Elroy?"

"Certainly, Colonel."

Sykes held up the cell phone. "Is this yours?"

"Well, I'll be damned," Elroy said. "Where did you find that? I've been looking for it for a week, maybe longer."

"It was found at the top of the hill out there."

"Well, I guess that's where I left it."

"Would you like it back?" Sykes held out the phone.

"I guess so, but I've already replaced it with an

iPhone." Elroy pressed the on button. "It's still dead."

"It was dead when you left it there?"

"Yeah, and it wouldn't take a charge. That's why I got a new one."

"Can I see the new one?"

"I didn't bring it today. What's the point? You've got no reception out here, anyway." He dropped the cell phone into his garbage can. "There's where it belongs," he said.

Sykes shrugged and left the room.

Bess passed through the kitchen.

"Bess?"

She stopped.

"Don't worry about your phone. It's in the garbage can."

She shrugged. "It's not mine," she said, then went on her way.

37

Bess sat in the living room, reading a book. Sykes usually turned in earlier than she, so she waited him out.

Sykes came in from his study. "You ready for bed?"

She ignored the double entendre. "Not yet. I'm into my book."

"Turn the lights off when you come up," he said, then went on his way.

She waited for another hour or so, and when no noises of movement came from upstairs, she got up, turned off all the lights, and waited a moment for her eyes to adjust to the darkness. She set her handbag near the bottom of the stairs, then removed a very small flashlight, the two trackers Tom had given her, and a folded piece of plastic sheeting from the bag. She listened for a moment, heard no more noises, then walked outside onto the porch. There was a clear sky and a quarter moon, enough to let her see the parked cars.

She waited a couple more minutes, then stepped off the porch, slipped out of her shoes, and walked over to where Sykes's Explorer was parked. She checked the upstairs windows for a light and found none, then listened again for noise and heard none. She walked to the rear of the Explorer, unfolded the plastic sheeting, hung one end around her shoulders, and fastened it into place with a snap. She lay down on the ground, maneuvered until her head was under the car, then held the little flashlight in her mouth and illuminated the underside of the car. She began moving backward, farther under the vehicle.

When the gas tank came into sight, she found a niche between that and the chassis and ripped the plastic tape off the tracker, marked number one, leaving an adhesive surface. She slipped the tracker into the niche and pressed it firmly in place for at least a minute, then she worked her way sideways from under the SUV.

She got up, walked over to the van, and repeated

her actions with the second tracker, marked number two, then wriggled out from underneath. She stood up, then brushed the dirt off the plastic sheet and off the seat and legs of her jeans. She was almost back to the porch when she heard footsteps from inside. She stepped into her shoes and quickly sat down in a rocking chair on the porch.

The door to the house opened and she turned her head to find Sykes standing there.

"What are you doing?" he asked.

"Enjoying the night air."

"You'll freeze your ass off out here."

"When I get cold, I'll come inside. What are you doing up?"

"I felt like one of Elroy's biscuits," he said. "I'll sleep better now."

"Good night, then."

"Good night." He went back inside and closed the door behind him.

She waited ten minutes, shivering in the dark, before she went up the hill to see if she'd had any e-mails. She had none, but she typed out one to the e-mail address with her father's name in it.

Dad, it read. Thank you for your kind gifts of the beautiful china pieces. I've put them in just the right spot in my living room. Love, Bess.

STUART WOODS

If anybody cared to look, there was a pair of china pieces on a bookcase in her apartment's living room.

Tom Blake sat down at his office desk and checked his iPhone for messages. The one from Bess stood out, and he was relieved to receive it. He switched on his computer and loaded the new tracking software, typing in the serial numbers of each of the trackers.

The map on the screen was of the continental forty-eight states, and at the press of a button, the software zoomed in closer, first to the state of Virginia, then to the location of the two trackers. He keyed in tight on the vehicles until he could see the symbols for the trackers. "Good," he said aloud to himself.

Then, as he watched, the SUV image began to move. He zoomed out half a mile or so and watched the car's progress as it drove toward the main road, then made a left turn toward the village a couple of miles away. He watched as the car drove into town and parked. He consulted a map to see that it was in front of a little grocery store. It stayed there for ten minutes or so, then began to move again.

The symbol for the SUV suddenly disappeared from the screen. Something was wrong. He zoomed out to a one-mile scale but could not recover the image. He superimposed the map of the village onto the tracking software and searched the main streets for the tracking symbol. Then, suddenly, it appeared in the lower, left-hand corner of the screen. It seemed to be leaving a gas station. That was it: he had stopped for gas and had been under a canopy for several minutes while he filled his tank.

Tom breathed a sigh of relief and went on with his work, but he left the tracking software on-screen until the vehicle was back in its usual parking spot at Sykes's compound.

Bess slept fairly late for her, making up the time lost in last evening's excursion. She missed breakfast, then after lunch climbed the hill again and perched on her favorite rock. Sykes came out of the house once with a pair of binoculars and trained them on her. She smiled and waved at him, then he went back inside.

At dinner, she was alone with Sykes; the others were apparently away from the compound. He turned on the TV for the evening news, and they both watched a story from the network's White House correspondent.

"The kerfuffle over the broken window at the White House is apparently over. The window has been replaced, and the staffer, who had minor cuts from the glass, is back at work." She returned the audience to the anchorwoman in the studio.

The anchorwoman continued, "President-elect Holly Barker has been spotted shopping on Madison Avenue in New York. A reporter who caught up with her got this comment."

They switched to a medium shot of Holly carrying shopping bags, and someone shouted a question at her from off camera.

"It's hard to campaign and shop at the same time, so I'm making it up today," Holly said, smiling at the camera.

Sykes switched off the television. He seemed annoyed.

"Had enough of the president-elect?" she asked Sykes.

"Not nearly enough," Sykes replied grumpily, and then changed the subject.

38

Tom Blake was at his desk when his secretary buzzed. "Yes?"

"Peg Parsons, on one."

Tom pressed the button. "Hi, Peg."

"You sound wary," she said.

"No, I don't. I may sound sleepy. I've been reading a very boring report."

"You don't have to be wary of me, Tom," she said. "I don't mind being an occasional piece of ass, but I'm not a home-wrecker."

"Not intentionally," he said, "but you have no idea how suspicious Amanda is when your name comes up."

"Then don't bring it up," she said.

"I make a point of not doing that."

"All right, all right. I have a tip for you. By the way, did your plan work when I published my piece?"

"It seemed to. I can't really go beyond that."

"Well, I have something new for you."

"Shoot."

"I can't shoot on the phone. Buy me lunch."

"That's dangerous, Peg, for both my case and my ass."

"Then cover them both, please, but we've had word that some of our lines at the paper are tapped, and we've been told to be careful what we say."

"Okay, lunch. But somewhere we won't be talked about if we're seen together."

"All right, we'll meet in my car at the same spot at Rock Creek Park—at the far end of the parking lot, away from the buildings. One o'clock?"

"Okay, at one."

"I'll bring lunch."

"See you then." He hung up and buzzed his secretary.

"Yes, sir?"

"I'm supposed to have lunch with Assistant Director Taylor today. Reschedule, will you? Tell him I have to see a source."

"Is Peg Parsons a source?"

"Don't you ever mention that name to anyone, understand?"

"Understood. I'll reschedule with Taylor." She hung up.

Tom arrived at Rock Creek Park first and parked where he had been told. She was right; that part of the lot was empty.

He switched off the ignition and waited. Two minutes later her little Mercedes parked alongside him, and she got out, carrying a wicker picnic basket. She didn't approach his car, she just walked into the woods, and he scurried after her.

There was no path, but the forest floor was covered in pine needles, so it was easy going. He began to hear the sound of flowing water, then he found her on a flat rock near the creek, and she was spreading a blanket.

"Hi, there," she said, opening the hamper and producing sandwiches, coleslaw, and a bottle of chardonnay. She handed him a corkscrew. "The wine is your job." She waved a hand: "Is this private enough?"

"It would seem so." He got the bottle open and filled the waxed paper cups she had brought.

She raised her cup. "Bon appétit. This is delicious, if I do say so."

He took a bite of his sandwich and drank some wine. "So, Peg, what have you got to tell me?"

"You know the group down in Virginia, the white-supremacy guys?"

"Maybe."

"Well, I now have a source on the inside, one who knows a lot about them."

"What has he told you?"

"I didn't say it was a 'he.' But for purposes of conversation, we'll assume the masculine pronoun."

"Sure."

"He hasn't been with them for all that long, but they're coming to trust him."

"How did he establish contact?"

"He got a call from a guy named Sykes, then they met."

"Is he participating in their, ah, adventures?"

"Not yet, but he believes he will be invited along soon. There was an incident with a cell phone, and that slowed things down, but he thinks they're back on track now. Apparently, the incident at the White House—broken window, injured staffer—was something to do with the group. He said that Sykes apparently thought they had killed Holly Barker, and when he saw her on TV, shopping in New York, he was upset to find she was still alive."

"I believe a decision was made to make it seem that she might have been sidelined."

"Hence, the story about the injured staffer?"

"Off the record, maybe something to do with that."

"Anyway, Sykes apparently believes that she's going to be in New York running her transition team, pretty much until the inaugural festivities."

"And he wants her in D.C., where she might be more accessible?"

"That's it, sweetheart."

"That's what you have to tell me?"

"Let's call it an introduction to my source."

"What's your source's name?"

"Can't tell you that."

"I need enough information about him to allow us to check him out. He could be a member of the group and just playing you."

She shook her head. "I did my own checking. He was a government employee before, so that made it easier."

He also needed enough information to ascertain whether Elizabeth Potter was her source as well as his. "I'm sorry, Peg. That's not how the Bureau works. If we're going to bring on a CI— a confidential informant—we have to do an FBI background check, and that's more thorough than you can imagine."

"Well, Tommy, that's not how it's going to work

with my source. He tells me, I tell you. If he turns out to be right, he's good. If not, well, you can look elsewhere. But I'm telling you, I have a very good nose, and if he was lying to me, I'd sniff him out. I don't need a platoon of FBI agents to do it for me."

"You're very cocky, aren't you?"

"Let's just say that I'm cock-oriented." She stroked his crotch and got a response.

"Careful," he said, "it bites."

"So do I," she said, pulling his zipper down and putting a hand inside to free him.

"Be gentle," he said, lying back and letting her have her way with him.

"Oh, that's right," she said. "You'll have to use it again tonight, won't you?" She went to work on him and got excellent results.

39

Tom sat at his desk, still a little weak in the knees, and tried to think how he might contact Elizabeth. He decided to continue to be Dad, e-mailing: Hi, there, baby. It's been too long since I've seen my girl. Let's get together soonest. When are you free? Love, Dad.

He pressed the send button. There was no way of telling when she'd see the e-mail; he'd just have to be patient. At five, he left the office and drove home. Amanda's car was in the garage, so he took a few deep breaths and put on his innocent face.

"Evening, sweetheart," he said, as he walked in.

Amanda looked up, surprised. "You're home early," she said. "To what do I owe the pleasure?" She kissed him and pressed herself against him.

"A long and very boring report," he said. "In fact, I think I need an hour's nap." He loosened his tie.

"Want some company?" she asked.

"Give me an hour, then I'm yours."

She checked her watch. "All right, you're on the clock. Shoo."

He went upstairs and got undressed. As he hung his suit on a hanger he saw something he hadn't seen before, and it scared him. The suit was a light tan, and there was lipstick on his fly.

He looked around for something that would dissolve lipstick. He went into the bathroom and found a bottle of rubbing alcohol and some tissues. He poured some on the Kleenex, replaced the bottle in the cabinet, then went back and applied it to his fly. To his vast relief it seemed to come off, but when he blew on it to dry it, it still left a visible stain, just not a red one. He hung the suit on the second rack, behind the first row, then flushed the tissues down the toilet.

Finally, he turned down the duvet, got into bed, and stretched out. In a couple of minutes he was snoring lightly.

———

He felt a draft and reached for the covers, but he encountered a head of hair instead. He hadn't inspected himself for lipstick stains, so he pulled her away and up to his lips.

"I smell alcohol," she said, sniffing.

"I spilt something on my suit at lunch, and I was trying to get out the stain."

She rolled on top of him and made to insert him. "You're not very responsive today," she said.

"I was sound asleep," he replied.

"Well, your hour is up." She fondled him until she got a response, then mounted him. Ten minutes later they were both spent. She went into the bathroom for a minute, then returned and opened his closet door. "Which suit? I'll see what I can do."

"The tan gabardine, second row."

She pulled it from the closet and hung it on a hook. "Where?"

"On the trousers," he said.

"What was the stain?"

"Russian dressing from a sandwich. That pink stuff." He held his breath.

"Yes, I can still smell the alcohol. And it seems to have worked." She put the suit back into the closet. "Dinner's in fifteen minutes," she said, pulling her jeans back on and slipping into a sweater and flip-flops. "See you downstairs."

Halfway through dinner his phone vibrated. "Excuse me," he said, and went to his messages.

Dear old Dad!

I'll be home around nine; if you can stop by, I'll give you a drink!

Your loving child

"Anything important?" Amanda asked.

"Yes, a message from a CI. He's not allowed to contact me by phone. I'll have to go out for an hour or so after dinner."

"Oh, well. At least I've already exhausted you. Don't fall asleep at the wheel."

Tom drove to Elizabeth's apartment house, near DuPont Circle, pulled into the garage, and parked. He took the elevator up to the floor above hers, then walked a flight down the fire stairs and peeked into the hallway. The coast was clear. He walked quickly down the hall, found the door off the latch, and let himself in. "Elizabeth?" he called.

"Have a seat. I'll be there in a minute."

He sat down on the sofa and looked around. He'd been there only once before, and it seemed much the same: comfortable.

Elizabeth appeared, buttoning her blouse.

"I hope I'm not interrupting anything," he said.

"Fat chance. Drink?"

"I've already had some wine with dinner. I'd better not."

She poured herself one and sat down. "What's up?"

"First, a question."

"Shoot."

"Have you recently had any contact with a female journalist?"

"You mean like Peg Parsons?"

"She'll do. Have you seen or communicated with her?"

"No, I haven't. Do you have some reason to believe that I might have?"

"I saw her today, and she told me that she has a source in Sykes's group."

"Holy shit."

"My feelings exactly. Do you have any idea who that might be?"

"Did she say it was a female?"

"No, she used the editorial male gender when speaking of him, but said it might be a woman."

"I'm the only woman I've seen there, so it's got to be a man. What sort of information did she get?"

"Nothing earthshaking. She said Sykes had seen Holly Barker in New York on television, so he knows she's not dead."

"I was with him at dinner when he saw that on TV."

"How did he react?"

"He seemed annoyed, but he didn't say anything more about her."

"I guess he wouldn't. I got your message about the trackers."

"Good."

"I checked them out, and they're working just fine. I watched his Explorer go into the village for groceries and gas, then return."

"That's odd," she said. "Elroy would ordinarily go in for groceries. Could it have been the liquor store? He might have bought some wine."

"Could be."

"Holy shit again!"

"What is it this time?"

"It's Elroy, the black cook."

"What about him?"

"He's got to be Peg Parsons's source!"

"Why do you say that?"

"Because he hates Sykes."

"How can you tell?"

"It's obvious, trust me."

"What's Elroy's last name?"

"Hubbard."

"Do you know anything about his background?"

"He's retired Navy, where he was a cook—supposedly his last posting was as the chef at the officers club at Naval Air Station Pensacola."

"I'll check him out," Tom said, glancing at his watch. "I've got to get home."

"Is Amanda keeping you on a short leash?"

"You could put it that way," he said.

She walked him to the door.

"Anything else to report?"

"Nope. Drive carefully." She let him out and locked the door behind him. She walked slowly back to the sofa. "Elroy," she said. "Now, whose team is he playing on?"

40

Tom found Amanda sound asleep, so he wouldn't have to make love for a third time today. He lay on his back, naked, cooling down, and thought about Elroy Hubbard.

Who did he represent in Sykes's camp?

There were options: he could simply be a source Peg Parsons had cultivated after a chance meeting. Or he could be CIA—they were never shy about trampling on his territory. Or one of the fifteen other intelligence agencies. Not the NSA: too technical. Then who would want what Hubbard had on Sykes? A state agency, maybe?

It took him an hour to sink into sleep, finally, after ten milligrams of Ambien. The following morning he was groggy, as he had known he would be after seeking pharmaceutical help so late. He took a cold shower to wake him sufficiently for action. But what action? He was running Elizabeth Potter as a one-off; there was no team to back her up, just himself. He contemplated creating a team, but he didn't want anyone to know he was running an agent alone—it would be embarrassing to ask for help at this late date, especially when the life of a president-elect was in play. And he didn't like admitting that he was working with the Secret Service, rather than with his own Bureau.

He called Mamie Short. She was experienced, inventive, and distrusted by most of the male agents because she was a female agent. There was still resistance to that in the Bureau.

He used his private line to call her on a direct line, avoiding secretaries.

"This is Short," she said.

"Mamie, Tom Blake. I need to see you outside the office, without our being seen together. Any suggestions as to where?"

"How about my office? This place empties out at noon, like a herd of cattle avoiding branding."

He thought about that; not a bad idea. "Is there a conference room with a lock on the door?"

"Two doors from my office." She gave him a room number. "Twelve-fifteen?"

"Good." He hung up.

At twelve-ten he walked two floors down the stairs and found the room. She was sitting at the table, munching on a sandwich.

"I brought you one," she said, indicating a brown paper bag at the next seat.

"Thanks, Mamie." He sat down and took a moment to think about her while unwrapping his sandwich. She was tallish, blond, early forties, casually dressed. Hoover would have hated her on sight.

"I've been running an agent on my own, and I need help."

"And you had to come two floors down to get that?"

"For a variety of reasons, I don't want to assemble a team."

"And you don't want to tell me what your reasons are?"

"If it becomes relevant, I will."

"Okay, I'll trust your judgment on relevance."

"Thank you. Do you know an agent named Elizabeth Potter?"

"Late twenties, a looker, smart?"

"That's a start."

"I met her once socially, and we had a little chat."

"How little?"

"Superficial, I should have said. She asked my advice."

"On what subject?"

"We had been talking about women in the Bureau, and she said, 'Any advice?' We were interrupted before I could give her any."

"There's a small group of white supremacists in Virginia, run by a man named Wade Sykes."

"Him, I've heard of: retired colonel, sort of drummed out of the Army for promoting his views too obviously."

"That's the one."

"How's Elizabeth doing?" Mamie asked.

"Pretty good: she's in, but our problem is communicating. There's no cell service at their compound and they only turn on the Wi-Fi twice a day, apparently at random times, so if I e-mail her, posing as her father, I never know when she'll get it."

"Okay, how can I help?"

"We've learned—let me rephrase that—we've heard from a journalist who has somebody inside, too. Elizabeth thinks she knows who—a black cook, using the name of Elroy Hubbard, whose legend is retired Navy cook, last assignment at Naval Air Station Pensacola, as chef at the officers club. I need you to run that name through the mill and see if that legend has roots, or is he just making it up. If somebody's running him, I want to know who, and I need at least one name."

"Okay, anything else?"

"Since what I've told you is everything, you and I know **everything** else."

"Why does Potter think he's Parsons's guy?"

"I didn't say it was Parsons."

"Oh, come on, Tom. You two were an item at Georgetown. I was there, too, remember?"

"Oh, yeah."

"Not that we knew each other well. Your time was taken up with Parsons."

"Okay, it's Peg. I have to keep that very quiet, because my wife's eyeballs bulge whenever her name is mentioned."

"Why are you even in touch with her?"

"I needed to plant a story in her column for cover."

"And she did that for you?"

"Yes."

"And what did she get out of it?"

"Mamie . . ."

"She had a reputation at Georgetown."

"Put her out of your mind," Tom said firmly. "Got it?"

"Okay, I'll use my imagination."

"Don't even do that."

Mamie recapped her pen. "Anything else?"

He scribbled a number on a blank card. "This is a burner phone. Leave a message there on how to reach you or see you."

She handed him a card. "No need. This is my burner."

Tom tucked it into a pocket.

"You want me to text you information?"

"If it's urgent. Otherwise, I'd rather talk face-to-face."

"You think you can read me better that way, Tom?"

"Don't be a smart-ass, Mamie."

"But I'm so good at it!"

"Thanks for the sandwich." He hadn't touched it. He put it back in the bag and took it with him, then ate it at his desk.

41

As Stone's G-500 pulled up to Jet Aviation at Teterboro, a three-car line of black SUVs rolled up to the wingtip. He turned to Holly. "Does the caravan mean you're not coming back to my house?"

"How observant you are," she said, pinching his cheek. "It's better if I establish a routine at the Carlyle and my transition office. Don't worry, I'll soon long for your touch."

"That can't come soon enough for me."

The stewardess opened the airstairs door and they parted at the bottom as Stone's luggage was loaded into the Bentley and Fred stood by. Holly was followed to the SUVs by her luggage and a large stack of cardboard cartons, looking like an attorney going to a very complicated trial. Soon, they were both on their way to the city by different routes, Holly via the George Washington Bridge, Stone via the Lincoln Tunnel.

Stone picked up the phone and called Dino.

"Bacchetti."

"It's Stone. I'm back from D.C. Dinner tonight at my place? I don't feel like a restaurant."

"As a matter of policy, I never turn down a free meal. Promise me a really good bottle of wine, and I'll stay the night."

"In that case, I'll promise you a bottle of mediocre wine. Six-thirty?"

"Done." Dino hung up.

Dino arrived on time and accepted a glass of his favorite Scotch in Stone's study. "So, why don't you feel like going to a restaurant? You eat nine of ten dinners out."

Stone sighed. "I don't know. Holly needed to be at the Carlyle, and I guess I wanted a more attractive date than you, if I were going to a restaurant. I have my reputation to think of."

"Which you so rarely do. Are you falling in love with Holly?"

"I think I fell in love with her at first sight, some years ago, but she has been only periodically available since that time, and I have to have a sex life to survive."

"I'm well aware. And Holly is an irregular lover?"

"Well put."

"Did you enjoy your stay at the White House?"

"No."

"Was the nation inattentive to your needs?"

"I prefer being the master in my own home to being a guest in the homes of others, even if my hosts are at the presidential level. Anyway, Holly was working like a beaver on policy papers and intelligence briefings. Oh, and there was an attempt on her life."

Dino's eyebrows went up. "Was that news report really about her?"

"Yes, except she wasn't wounded. The Secret Service and the FBI had a dummy built and set up in front of a window."

"How did the dummy do?"

"She took two in the head," Stone replied. "And that through a window I would have presumed to be bulletproof."

"Technology fails again."

"Well, yes. So, where most people would keep

their heads down after such an experience, Holly prefers being a moving target, with somewhat more Secret Service protection."

"As the comedian Brother Dave Gardner used to say, 'Everybody to his own kick.'"

"I believe he did."

"So where does that leave you? Unfucked?"

"Until Holly can't stand it anymore and bails out of the Carlyle."

"Well, you've always considered yourself a serial monogamist, Stone. Someone usually turns up when you're in need."

"I'm uncomfortable with that, as long as Holly and I are in the same city."

"So now you're geographically monogamous?"

"For lack of a better term."

Dinner arrived and they sat down and were served by Fred.

"It bothers me," Stone said.

"That you're geographically monogamous?"

"Yes. It's a new experience."

"Well, you could always surprise Holly at the Carlyle."

Stone shook his head. "She'd be in the middle of interviewing a candidate for secretary of defense, or some such. I'd need an appointment to see her."

"Sort of takes the thrill out of it, huh?"

"How do you handle Viv being gone so much?"

"I save up my energy and my precious bodily fluids for her return."

"Would she mind if you saw someone else while she's away?"

"Only if she knew about it. The woman is armed, you know."

"There is that."

"Anyway, I'm content with things as they are. If she were home all the time I'd be exhausted every morning, and my weight loss would make my suits too big. I couldn't afford the alterations."

After dinner they took chairs by the fireplace, and Stone poured them brandy. "I'm glad you don't smoke cigars," he said, handing Dino a snifter.

"Right back atcha. What would you do, if you met a highly desirable woman who smoked cigars?"

"Deny her access to the house," Stone replied without hesitation. "And my body."

"It's going to be interesting to see how you handle Holly's transition period," Dino said. "And even more interesting after she takes office."

"I don't even want to think about that," Stone said.

"Well, after January 20 you'll at least have solved the geographical monogamy issue."

"Let's hope you're right," Stone said. "Though the resolution will not be in my favor. I have already told her that I will **not** move into the White House."

"But you will visit, occasionally?"

Stone shrugged. "I'll probably keep a pinstriped suit and a tuxedo there."

"Careful, Stone, you're edging toward commitment."

"Don't worry, I'll stay well back from the brink."

"Surely, there are some advantages to living in the White House."

"Well, let's see: I'd be awakened in the middle of the night whenever she receives a phone call about an emergency. I can't think of any others."

"I understand the service is pretty good."

"It's better at my house," Stone said.

42

There was a note on Tom Blake's desk to call Mamie Short. He did so.

"Same as before?" she asked.

"Right. Five minutes." They hung up and he walked downstairs to her conference room and locked the door behind him. "Good morning. Did you find out about Elroy Hubbard?"

"Well, I had a dream," she said.

"Do I look like Sigmund Freud?"

"No, no cigar. It was more of what you might call a reality dream."

"Spit it out, Mamie."

"Did I ever tell you I was employed at the CIA for a couple of years?"

"No, but it's in your file. You were unhappy there, I believe."

"It was more like they were unhappy with me," she said. "Anyway, during my training at the Farm, there was a black guy named Leroy Collins in my class. What I remember about him was that he was good at everything he did, and also he was a good cook. He specialized in Southern cooking, which he said he'd learned from his mother, and he made dinner for a bunch of us a couple of times."

"So you think that Leroy Collins is now Elroy Hubbard?"

"I think it's a good enough guess for you to check it out with the Agency before I spend any more time identifying him. Don't you?"

"I'll get back to you," Tom said, then went back to his office and called the director of central intelligence, Lance Cabot.

"Good morning, Tom," Lance said.

"Good morning, Lance."

"I've got a meeting in half a minute, but if this is important, I'll hold them at bay for you."

"Thank you. I believe you have an operative imbedded with a white-supremacist group down in Virginia, posing as a retired Navy cook."

Lance was silent while he apparently tried and

failed to figure out why Tom had this information. "Anything is possible," he said, finally.

"In that case, I have some information you might find interesting. Are you available for lunch?"

"I am, if we do it at Langley. Anyway, we have a better chef here than you do at the Bureau."

"We don't have a chef," Tom replied.

"My very point. One o'clock?"

"See you then."

They both hung up.

Tom was waved through the gate at Langley; he had been there before. He liked visiting the Agency; it was a brighter workplace than the Hoover building, and the people seemed smarter than most of his agents.

He was issued a visitor's pass at the reception desk, and a uniformed guard walked him to the elevator and rode up with him to the executive floor. Lance's secretary met him and walked him to a small sitting room adjacent to Lance's office, where a table had been set for two. She inquired if he would like a drink, and he requested iced tea. He was halfway through the glass before Lance swept in.

"So sorry to be tardy, Tom, but there is always someone wanting to save lives and needing my permission."

"I know the feeling," Tom replied, shaking the offered hand.

Lance waved him to a seat at the table, where a cold soup had already been served. "Tom, I don't mind telling you that I am deeply concerned that your people have unearthed our man in Virginia."

"Relax, Lance," Tom said. "He isn't exactly blown, so you needn't be worried."

"Just what, exactly, does 'isn't exactly blown' mean?"

"Well, and what a coincidence, we have an operative inside, as well."

"How did Collins reveal himself to this gentleman?"

"He didn't. And I may as well tell you, the gentleman is a lady. She's been with the Bureau for twelve years, and her cover is that she's secretary to a deputy attorney general."

"Well, we seem to have our Colonel Sykes boxed, don't we?" Lance said with obvious pleasure.

"I'm not sure about that," Tom said.

"Why not? How many more people do we need on this?"

"Because we can't prove he's done what he's done. At least not yet."

"Well, we know he did the Maine murders."

"Knowing is not the same as proving. At the Bureau, we have to do both."

"How about this business at the White House earlier this week?"

"There are other problems there as well," Tom said.

"I was afraid there might be," Lance said. He picked up his soup by the two handles on the bowl and drank it down. "Go on, enlighten me further."

"Not surprisingly, Sykes doesn't trust your man because he's black."

"Is your agent white?"

"Yes."

"Well, that's a relief."

"Not really."

"Now what?"

"She's told Sykes that she's a lesbian—to keep his hands off her. And for Sykes, that's at about the same level as being black."

"Oh, dear. He's not trusting either of them, then?"

"Correct."

"What has your agent accomplished so far?"

"Well, she managed to get word to us that the White House event was upcoming, but communications from that compound are problematical, and her message was garbled. We managed to head them off, though. We set up a dummy in a window, and they took that out."

"Oh, good."

"But we still can't prove anything. We don't even have enough for a search warrant, and now they know that Holly is still alive."

"Has your girl made contact with Collins?"

"Yes, but they don't know each other's identities."

"Well, as long as we both have people there we ought to arrange for them to work together, ought we not?"

"We ought."

"How should we accomplish that?"

"Let's each send a message to our respective operative, tell him or her who the other is, and ask them to have a heart-to-heart talk," Tom said.

"What name is your operative using?" Lance asked, pen poised over his notebook.

"Bess Potts."

"And her actual name?"

"Elizabeth Potter."

"Consider it done," Lance said.

"I'll inform Elizabeth at the first opportunity."

"All right, then."

Lance's secretary came into the room. "Director, I'm afraid . . ."

"Say no more," Lance said, rising. "Tom, I'm needed. Finish your lunch at your leisure."

"Thank you, Lance," Tom said, rising and shaking his hand.

Lance fled.

Tom stopped at a fast-food restaurant on the way back to his office and had a burger.

43

Tom was still on the road back to D.C. when his phone rang.

"A.D. Blake?"

"Yes."

"The director for you."

"All right."

There was a click. "Tom?"

"Yes, sir."

"Where are you?"

"On the way in from Langley. I had lunch with Lance Cabot, sort of."

"The Secret Service detail for our boss-to-be has requested a meeting in New York. There's a chopper waiting for you on the pad. It may be overnight."

"Yes, sir."

"I'll let Bill Wright know. You're meeting at a house in Turtle Bay." He gave the address. "It belongs to Stone Barrington, whom I think you've met."

"Yes, sir."

"A car will meet you at the East Side Heliport."

"Thank you, sir."

But the director had already hung up.

Tom called home and Amanda answered. "Hey, there."

"Hi, what's up?"

"I have to go to New York for a couple of days."

"Why?"

"I can't say on the phone. Will you pack me a bag, and I'll tell you when I get there."

"Sure. How much stuff?"

"A suit and a blazer and three of everything else. I'll be there in twenty minutes." He hung up.

Amanda was standing in the driveway, next to a suitcase, when he pulled up. She tossed it into the rear seat, then got in up front. "Okay, why?"

"The Secret Service has requested a meeting on the subject of Holly Barker."

"What else?"

"That's all I know."

"Well, shoot! I wanted more than that."

"Think of it this way: you won't have to keep any secrets."

"I **like** knowing secrets."

"I'll tell you everything when I get back."

"Oh, all right."

He kissed her and reversed out of the driveway. A half hour later he was on a helicopter to New York.

When he landed, to Tom's astonishment, Bill Wright was standing on the helipad, leaning on a Bentley. A minute later they were underway.

"Clearly, Bill," Tom said, "I'm working for the wrong federal agency."

"The car belongs to Stone Barrington, and this is his driver, Fred."

"Hello, Fred."

"Sir, welcome aboard," Fred replied. "We'll be there in ten minutes."

"Stone and I thought it would be preferable to conduct our business at his house, rather than flock to the Carlyle, where Ms. Barker is residing."

"Oh? From what I saw at the White House, I thought they were occupying the same bed."

"Well, yes, when she can get away. That will all have to change after she's inaugurated, of course. But until then, I have to employ persuasion to keep her alive."

"I should think that's how you'll have to do it when she's living in the White House, too," Tom said.

"Perhaps I can train her a little."

"Good luck with that."

They drove into a garage and got out of the car. "Fred will put your bag in your room," Bill said. "We're meeting in Stone's office. This way."

Stone looked up to see the two federal agents walk into his office. He offered them seats and coffee.

"Your meeting, Bill," he said, when they were situated.

"Sykes is on the move," Bill said, "and we don't know where."

Tom set his briefcase on the coffee table and pulled out his laptop. "Give me a moment, and I'll tell you where they are," he said.

"You've got a tracer on them?"

"One on Sykes's Ford Explorer, another on their van." He kept typing. "Ah, here we are," he said. "Both vehicles are driving north on the interstate."

"Sounds like they're heading for New York," Bill said.

"Well, we got here first."

"Suppose they are headed here?" Stone said. "What's your plan?"

"I don't have one," Tom said. "An hour ago, I didn't know I was headed here. Bill, what's **your** plan?"

"My plan is to move Peregrine back to this house."

"Peregrine?"

"That's our service's temporary code name. Perhaps when she's in office we'll come up with something more elegant."

"I like your plan," Stone said. "We can put up you and Claire, too."

"We accept with thanks," Bill said. "Excuse me a moment." He got out his phone and pressed a button. "Ma'am, what time will you be finished at the transition office? Very good. I'm afraid we're going to have to move you to the Barrington house for the night—maybe more than one. Claire can pick up whatever you need from the Carlyle. I'll explain later. Yes, ma'am." He hung up. "She was surprisingly willing to make the move."

"I'm pleased to hear it," Stone said. "Now, what's your plan?"

"To secure her in this house," Bill replied. "After that it will depend on where she has to be and when. There's no telling. Also we have to divine the intentions of Colonel Sykes."

Tom spoke up. "I should tell you both, in the strictest confidence, that we have an operative in Sykes's group."

"Very good!" Wright said.

"I should also tell you that the CIA has one there, too."

"A wealth of riches," Stone said.

"Not exactly," Tom said. "Communications are difficult, and I don't even know yet if the CIA plant has been told about our agent. We have to wait to hear from one or both of them."

"Is one of them in Sykes's car?"

"We don't know, but we doubt that Elroy Hubbard is. That's the cover name for Sykes's cook."

"Then we'll wait," Stone said.

44

Bess had been told by Sykes at breakfast that she was traveling with him to New York within the hour.

"For how long?" she asked.

"Don't get nosy," he replied.

"A girl has to know what to pack."

"What have you got here?" he asked.

"Clothes for a couple of days."

"Then that will have to do you. We're not making any stops. You can shop in New York, if you need more."

"Where are we staying?"

"You and I will be at the Lowell, on East Sixty-third, on Madison Avenue. The others will be nearby."

"I don't know the Lowell."

"It's enough that I do," he said. "Ask Elroy to fix us some sandwiches. I'd like a ham on rye. You and the others can tell him what you want."

After breakfast she walked into the kitchen. Elroy was making his daily biscuits. He walked to the sink, beckoned to her, and turned on the water, the force of which made a drumming noise when it struck the steel sink. He leaned in to her ear.

"I know who you are, Ms. Potter, and that Tom Blake sent you here. I'm CIA. I thought you should know."

She was not stunned. "We're going to New York today, and we'll need to pack a lunch: the colonel wants a ham on rye, and I'd like chicken on whole grain, with mayo."

Elroy nodded. "I know what the others will want. I'll bring it out to you at the car; fifteen minutes."

Bess went up to her room and packed the things she had just unpacked. She took her bag downstairs and found Elroy waiting for her with two bags. "Don't talk," he said, handing her a bag.

"Okay, thanks for the sandwiches."

She put her bag in the luggage compartment and the lunch on the floor of the rear seat, where she could reach it.

Sykes came out of the house, motioned her into the Explorer, and got in behind the wheel. Four others were getting into the van. Eugene and Earl were among them. The other two were Rod and Jimmy, to whom she had barely spoken.

Sykes drove away in silence. Soon they were on the interstate, driving north.

"You know," Bess said, "when you invited me aboard I thought that you had some respect for my intelligence."

"What makes you think I don't?" Sykes asked.

"Your reluctance to confide the details of what we're doing. I don't like working in the dark."

"You should know by now that I'm very security-conscious."

"Obviously. Are the others better informed than I?"

"I inform whoever, whenever I think they need to know. You and I aren't there yet, but will be fairly soon, I suspect."

Bess thought it was time to press the point. "I just want you to know that I'm through taking blind orders. If you don't feel you can confide in me, then just drop me at the nearest place I can get a cab or a bus, and I won't trouble you further. You needn't be concerned about me talking, since I don't know anything."

There was a long silence. "Fair enough," he said finally.

She took a deep breath and let it out slowly. Finally, she would make some progress.

"There's a rest stop a couple of miles up the road. I'll drop you there, and you can call a cab."

"As you wish," she said, steadying her voice so as not to sound disappointed.

He pulled into the rest stop and parked. "Go use the ladies' room. When you come back, I'll brief you. Take ten minutes. I want to talk to the lads."

"Shall I take my luggage?"

"You can leave it here. I trust you, Bess."

"Thank you." She got out of the Explorer and went into the ladies' side of the restroom. She checked all the booths, then locked herself into the one farthest from the sink, got out her burner phone, and called Tom Blake's burner.

"Yes?"

"It's me," she said.

"I'm relieved to hear it."

"Listen. I'm going to talk fast because I may be interrupted."

"I know you're at a rest stop."

"Right. I had forgotten. We're headed for New York. Sykes and I are staying at the Lowell on East Sixty-third Street. He wouldn't tell me what he's planning, so I said if he didn't trust me I wanted out. Now he says he does. Elroy, the cook, told me he's with another agency. Do you know if that's true?"

"It is. His name is Leroy Collins, and he's CIA."

"Good. We didn't have a chance to talk further."

"Why are you going to New York?"

"Sykes relented and said he would brief me when I get back into the car. Should I continue?"

"Yes. I've no reason to believe you're in danger. I'm in New York. When you learn your room number at the Lowell, leave a message for me, and I'll send you some things."

She checked her watch. "I have to go now."

"Right. I'll try to arrange a meeting."

"Okay." She hung up and tucked the phone in the lining of her handbag, then she flushed the toilet and left the booth. There was one elderly woman in the restroom, washing her hands.

Tom made a phone call. "Sykes and Bess will be staying at the Lowell Hotel, Sixty-third and

Madison. I want the manager visited personally by a senior agent, who should work to gain the cooperation of that person to the extent of getting video and audio equipment installed. He should also rent an adjoining room or suite or, if one is not available, urge the transfer of another guest. That failing, take the nearest space available. Apply for a search warrant immediately. You have less than two hours before their arrival." He hung up.

Sykes had the motor running when she got back to the car. In a minute, they were back on the interstate, with the van following. "Did you talk to the boys?" she asked.

"I did."

"What did you tell them?"

"I told them that I trust you and that you are an equal member of our team."

"To whom does the team report?"

"To me."

"And to whom do you report?"

He hesitated for a moment. "I report directly to God," he said, finally.

"Oh, good. I'd like to sit in on your next meeting."

"Trust me, he wouldn't like you."

"Because I'm a lesbian?"

"Among other things."

"What are the other things?"

"Mainly, your tendency to ask too many questions," he said firmly.

They drove on in silence.

45

Stone was still meeting with Tom Blake and Bill Wright when a small, red light blinked over the door that led to the garage. "She's here," Stone said.

They all got to their feet a second before Holly bustled in, carrying shopping bags. "Evening, all," she said. "Who do I have to beat up to get a drink around here?"

"That would be me," Stone said, moving to the bar. "But be gentle."

"Some of that filthy bourbon you drink," she said.

Stone poured them both one.

"Gentlemen," Holly said, "I command you to drink an alcoholic beverage."

"As long as you put it that way," Tom said. "I'll try your bourbon, too, Stone."

"As will I," Bill said.

The door opened and Claire Dunn entered, carrying more shopping bags. She had become the de facto bodyguard for Holly.

"You're drinking, too, Claire," Holly said.

"It's an order from the top," Bill said.

Claire dropped her bags. "Can you make a martini, Stone?"

"It's one of my many virtues," Stone replied, then reached into a freezer drawer for a bottle he had premixed and poured her one. He dropped two olives stuffed with anchovies into the glass and handed it to her.

Bill raised his glass. "The next administration," he said, and they all drank.

Holly took the chair next to Stone's. "If we're going to talk shop, we'd better do it before the booze kicks in," she said.

"Tom," Bill said, "you're here to fill us in on your end."

"Fortunately, I have more to report than I would have had a few hours ago," Tom said. "To sum it up, we're dealing with a five-man unit of domestic terrorists who have apparently been organized for the express purpose of preventing the president-elect from becoming president. Their leader is a retired Army colonel, Wade Sykes, who resigned from the service under a cloud when he was found to be distributing white-supremacist literature among some of his command. There are four other members residing at his compound in Virginia. We have first names only: Eugene, Earl, Rod, and Jimmy. There are also two others who are not residents there but visit regularly. One of them, unbeknownst to Sykes, is a female special agent of the FBI; the other is an African-American who cooks at the compound and is a member of the CIA."

"What interest does the CIA have in all this?" Bill asked. "They're off their turf, aren't they?"

"I had lunch today with Lance Cabot to ask him just that, but I failed in my mission when lunch was cut short."

"As lunch with Lance often is," Stone remarked.

"Since Stone is a special advisor to Lance," Tom said, "I will ask him to get us an answer to that question."

"I'll do my best," Stone said.

"Thus far, there have been three attempts on the president-elect's life. All, I'm glad to say, have been unsuccessful. You all know about the Maine incident and last week's shooting of the dummy in the family quarters of the White House."

There was a murmur of assent.

"There was also a failed attempt at Ms. Barker's Georgetown residence, in which our female agent took part as the getaway driver."

"What have the two operatives at the compound learned?"

"Elizabeth Potter, who is known as Bess Potts at the compound, gleaned sufficient knowledge to foil the Georgetown and White House attacks, but she was not yet a member of the group at the time of the Maine incident. We have not yet had a report from the cook, Leroy Collins, known at the compound as Elroy Hubbard. Sykes does not trust him, apparently because he's black, but fortunately, he likes the man's cooking.

"As we speak, Sykes, Bess, and the four other members are on their way to New York, apparently for another attempt. This time, we hope we will have enough intelligence to bag them all. We are helped by the fact that Bess has managed to plant trackers on both the vehicles they are traveling in: a Ford Explorer and a van." He turned his laptop around so that they could see the screen. "As you can see, they're in New Jersey now.

"Sykes and Bess are staying at the Lowell Hotel on East Sixty-third at Madison. We hope to penetrate their quarters. We're seeking a search warrant now. That's about it."

"All that is encouraging," Bill said, "but we still don't have enough evidence to arrest them for anything."

"I know, and that's discouraging," Tom replied.

Stone spoke up. "A question that hasn't been asked or answered is whether this is a small band of people working on their own, or are they part of a larger group?"

"I'm afraid none of us has anything on that," Bill said.

Holly spoke up. "Gentlemen—and Claire—do any of you have an opinion of the group's chances of succeeding?"

There was dead silence for a count of about ten while each of the participants hoped someone else would say it, then Stone spoke up. "A president, I think Harry Truman, said that anyone could kill a president, as long as he was willing to die himself."

"I think that's close to being the truth," Bill said. "But certain precautions can make a difference. For example, ma'am, at every rally you've attended while under our protection, from the beginning of your campaign until the present, all the people in the first three rows of the crowd have

CHOPPY WATER

been prescreened. Most of them were campaign
workers or volunteers known to the local orga-
nizers. We've collected the names, dates of birth,
and Social Security numbers of all the others and
run them through a computer program designed
to reveal if any of them have been treated for a
serious mental condition, or is known to have
committed a violent crime, including domestic
violence, or has threatened the life of a president.
By thus cleansing the first three rows of such
people, attempts on the principal's life has been
sharply reduced, as long—and this is essential—
as the principal does not penetrate the crowds.

"A training film exists of a campaign appearance
by former Alabama governor George Wallace, in
which he ignores that stricture and spontaneously
plunges into the crowd, shaking their outstretched
hands. Just beyond the third row he encounters
one Arthur Bremer, who shoots him five times
before our people can reach him, thereby instantly
turning Mr. Wallace into a paraplegic, wheelchair
bound for the remainder of his life."

"I've seen that film," Holly said, "and it put
the fear of God into me—or, at least, the fear of
crowds."

"I'm very glad to hear that, ma'am, because that
fear may save your life."

"I think the real moral of that story," Stone said, "is listen to and obey the Secret Service."

"I shall endeavor to do so," Holly replied. "Up to a point."

"Ah," Bill Wright said. "That point where you are, however briefly, on your own."

46

Tom Blake was shown to his room and, before showering and changing, made a call. "What is your progress?" he asked.

"The manager at the hotel declined to cooperate until shown a search warrant," the agent said. "It arrived ten minutes ago, and we are now in the suite."

"How much time do you need?"

"Fifty minutes," he said.

"Call the superintendent of the New Jersey state police, describe the two vehicles, and ask him to have his people stop and inspect half a dozen vehicles, among them the suspects'. Tell him this is at the request of the director and the attorney general."

"Is that a fact, sir?"

"It will be by the time they are stopped. Goodbye."

Tom called the director, made his case, got his approval, then asked him to call and alert the attorney general. He phoned his agent again. "You are now officially authorized. What is your progress?"

"We need another forty minutes," the man replied. "Our equipment shows the vehicles twelve minutes out from the Lincoln Tunnel."

"You'll make it. You know, of course, that if Sykes twigs to your installation, you'll be taken out and shot."

"Of course, sir. If I fail, I'll look forward to that."

The group gathered downstairs for dinner in the dining room, prepared by Stone's cook, Helene, and served by her husband, Fred.

"What news, Tom?" Bill Wright asked.

Tom looked at his watch. "Our suspect vehicles were delayed at the New Jersey end of the Lincoln Tunnel, where a number of cars were stopped and inspected. It cost them twenty minutes of travel time, so they should be arriving at the Lowell just about now."

CHOPPY WATER

Bess was impressed that they were met at curbside by not just a bellman but the hotel manager, who greeted Sykes by name and rank. "We have a very nice suite for you," he said, "and the young lady is nearby. We need ten minutes for the maids to finish. May I get you some refreshment?"

Bess asked for iced tea, and the colonel, bourbon, and they were steered to a seating area.

"I don't like the delay," Sykes said.

"Who does? This happens to me at least half the time when I'm traveling."

"Well, it doesn't happen to me," Sykes said, sourly.

After five minutes the manager returned and walked them to the elevator and all the way to their accommodations.

Bess was put into a small double room next door to Sykes's suite, with instructions to go there for a drink at seven. They would go out to dinner after that.

As soon as the bellman and the manager left, she began unpacking. There was a light rap on the door. She opened it to find an empty hallway, then she heard the rap again. She closed the door and went to another door, from whence the rapping was coming. She unlocked it, and the door was opened by a tall man in a dark suit.

"Ah, Special Agent Potter," he said, pulling her into his room and closing the door behind her. "I'm Fisk."

"Bess Potts, from here on," she said, shaking his hand. "What preparations have you made?"

"His suite is wired to the gills, and shortly, so will you be."

"You expect me to wear a wire?"

"No, I expect you to wear a string of pearls," he said, opening a jewelry box and removing it. "They were your grandmother's, except one is a microphone and quite undetectable. The antenna is what the pearls are strung on, and the receiver and transmitter are in the clasp."

"How do I turn it on?" she asked.

He opened another box. "By squeezing an earring," he said, showing her a pair, "in your right earlobe. Your grandmother's, too." He showed her the clasp of the necklace, and she put it on, then the earrings, each a pearl. "Try it."

She squeezed the right earring and was surprised that it gave to her touch.

"Up and running," another agent said, consulting his computer.

"How long are they good for?"

"Three to four hours," he said, turning the gear off for her. "If he leaves you for a few minutes, turn it off and save the juice, but don't forget to turn it back on."

"Got it. I've got to get dressed." She went back to her room and locked the door behind her. She heard it lock again from the other room.

She got into the only dress she had, changed her shoes, brushed her hair, and applied makeup lightly, then she put on the pearls and earrings. She turned them on and then presented herself at the door next to hers, using the knocker at seven sharp.

Sykes was wearing a suit when he admitted her. "How lovely you look," he said. "And pearls!"

"They were my grandmother's," she said. "I wear them occasionally."

One of Sykes's men, Jimmy, stepped in from another room.

"Okay, Bess," Sykes said. "Strip off."

She returned a level gaze. "What did you say to me?"

"I said, take your clothes off. Jimmy's got to check you for a wire."

"You first," she said, firmly. "Jimmy, too."

Sykes glared at her. "Do as I say."

"No," she replied. "I don't strip on any man's command."

"I can use the wand," Jimmy said.

"All right," Sykes replied, "use the wand."

Bess pretended to scratch her ear and squeezed the right earring, turning off the receiver/transmitter. She spread her arms wide and allowed Jimmy to pass the wand over her entire body, including her crotch, then she put her hands down. "You're done," she said.

"Just your shoes to go," he replied.

She held up each shoe for him to check. "Now," she said, "who do I have to kill to get a drink?" Sykes turned toward the bar tray, and she squeezed the earring again, turning the wire back on. Her blood pressure was up, and she was panting slightly. She sat down and took a few slow, deep breaths, then resumed breathing normally. "So," she said, "what does the evening hold for us?"

"Not much," Sykes said. "Just changing American history."

"Oh, I want to hear all about that," she said cheerfully.

47

Tom Blake excused himself to answer his phone. "Yes?"

"It's Fisk, sir. Sykes had her checked for a wire, but she turned off the system before the wand could pick it up. He's talking to her," the man said, "but they're leaving now."

"Tell the man downstairs to wait until they're in a cab. Then get into his suite and go over it with a fine-tooth comb, but **very** carefully. Don't leave a hair out of place." He hung up and returned to the table. "Our agent's wire is working. They're leaving the hotel now to go to dinner somewhere. They'll be followed."

"Are FBI agents sneaky enough for this kind of

work?" Stone asked. "I always think of them in double-breasted suits and fedoras."

"That's only in the noir movies of the forties and fifties," Tom replied. "We run more to blue blazers, tweed jackets, and khakis now. Beards, too."

Tom's phone rang again, and he made to get up, but Stone gestured him to sit. "You might as well sit and put it on speakerphone," he said.

Tom set the phone down and pressed the speaker button. "Yes? We're all listening."

"They didn't take a cab," the agent said. "Sykes was heard telling the manager that they were going to Rotisserie Georgette, which is within walking distance."

"I know the place," Stone said. "Where would you like them to sit?"

"At the back of the room," the agent replied. "We already have a man and a woman at the end of the bar."

"You want them near Sykes?"

"Yes, sir, if possible."

Stone called the restaurant. "Georgette?"

"Stone? What time should we expect you?"

"Not tonight, but there are some people on the way I'd like you to seat at the rear of the room, but away from the kitchen. His name is Sykes.

And there's a couple at that end of the bar that I'd like near them before they arrive."

"Certainly."

"And, please, keep it to yourself."

"Of course. We look forward to seeing you soon."

"Maybe tomorrow," he said, "if the stars align."

"See you then."

Stone hung up. "They'll be placed as you wished," he said to Tom.

"I don't know why it isn't always this easy," Tom said.

"I'd love to dine there tomorrow evening," Holly said. "And that would give Tom the opportunity to case the joint ahead of our arrival."

Sykes and Bess arrived at Rotisserie Georgette in due course, and they were seated at the rear of the restaurant at a corner table. They ordered drinks, then Sykes swept the room with his eyes while Bess looked at the menu.

"See anybody suspicious?" she asked.

"Not yet. Order for the two of us."

"That's easy. Looks like the specialty of the house is roast chicken." She ordered the food and wine.

Sykes continued to look at every table anywhere near them.

"I think the couple behind you must be going through a divorce," he said.

"How can you tell?"

"They're talking to each other."

Bess laughed.

Finally, he turned his attention to her. "The boys are going to have to get used to you," he said. "They're unaccustomed to meeting the needs of women."

"Then I'll help them out," Bess said. "By the way, how are you planning to change history with only four men and a woman to help you?"

"History moves in inches," he said. "But sometimes with a big step."

"How big are we talking?"

"I think you know who we're talking about. You visited her home briefly."

"Ah, that would be a big step, and I wouldn't be sorry to see her take it."

"You may have that opportunity. If everybody, including you, does his job well, no one will even notice that it was done but our masters."

"Masters? Sounds fascinating," she said.

Any reply was interrupted by the arrival of their first course. Then Sykes stopped talking and started eating.

"They're eating," Tom said, "and Sykes isn't talking."

"Are your agents getting a divorce?" Stone asked.

Tom laughed. "They'd have to get married first."

Bess restrained herself from asking further questions for the rest of dinner; instead, she just let him ramble on about the Army, about dealing with Washington, about hunting and fishing—whatever crossed his mind. He became more relaxed as the evening wore on and the level in the wine bottle went down. He mentioned her lesbianism only once, and in regretful terms. She reflected that telling him that had been one of her best decisions, as it kept him off her back without arguments.

"Where'd you find the boys?" she asked, while they were waiting for the check.

"They all served under me in the Army," Sykes replied. "The best of the best, especially Eugene, who is the best shot with a rifle I ever saw."

"Are there more of them than I've met?"

"Let's just say we have ample backup, should we need it."

"Who are my orders coming from? You? Or someone further up the line?"

"That's a bold question, and I won't answer it now."

"So you still don't trust me?"

"Trust has many levels."

"Where am I on the scale?"

"Let me ask you a question that might answer your question," Sykes said.

"All right."

"When everything is ready, will you be willing to pull the trigger yourself?"

Bess thought about that for a minute, just to make him think she was considering it. "Well," she said, finally, "I think I would be able to do that, but it remains to be seen, doesn't it?"

"And, based on your response, where would you put yourself on the scale when it comes to trust?"

"At better than ninety-nine percent, I think."

"Then I'll trust you all the way to ninety-nine percent," Sykes said.

"But not one hundred percent?"

"That remains to be seen, doesn't it?"

48

The group sat around Stone's dining table, a large pot of coffee on the table, and listened to the transmission.

"That was live," Tom Blake said, when there was no further conversation from the restaurant.

"I suppose we couldn't expect her to say one hundred percent, when she knew she was being recorded," Stone said.

"On the contrary," Tom replied. "She's certainly willing to lie to him, and any court would believe her when she testified she was lying. She's keeping him on edge. She doesn't want him to be entirely comfortable with her."

"Why not?" Bill Wright asked.

"Because she believes if he's on edge he'll be more likely to make mistakes," Tom replied. "Hang on, they're walking back to the Lowell now."

The group quieted down and listened.

"Wade," Bess said, "when are we expected to pull this thing off?"

"They'll accept my judgment on that. They know that I'm not suicidal, that I will expect to walk away when it's done. I want to be sure you'll walk away, too."

"Thank you for that," she said. "That's pretty much how I feel, too."

He laughed. "Then neither of us is suicidal."

"I guess not." They walked a little farther. "How about Eugene? Is he suicidal?"

"That's an interesting question," he muttered, half to himself. "On a battlefield, Eugene would walk into gunfire."

"But where is this battlefield going to be?"

"In an urban area with a good-sized audience, probably. Depends on where the target moves."

"Will Eugene walk into gunfire in those circumstances?"

"I believe he would. He believes too deeply in his principles to allow himself to walk away."

"Where did he acquire those principles?" she asked.

"From me," Sykes replied.

They reached the Lowell and stopped talking as they crossed the lobby. They remained quiet in the elevator, too.

"Good night," Sykes said when they reached their floor.

"Good night," Bess replied, letting herself into her room.

She listened at the door for a minute, then crossed the room and rapped on the door to the adjoining suite.

Fisk opened the door. "You okay?" he asked, regarding her closely.

"I'm just fine," she said. "Did you get it all?"

"Every word," he replied.

"Then I'm going to bed," she said, closing the door and locking it behind her. She took off the necklace and earrings and left them on a charging pad Fisk had given her. Then she took off her clothes, got into a nightgown, and went to bed.

All right," Tom said to the group. "It's a conspiracy, and a wider one than Sykes and his four men."

"I agree," Bill said, "judging from the way Sykes talked. He referred to his 'master' or 'masters' in the plural. And he didn't deny that his orders came from somewhere above."

Everybody muttered in agreement.

Claire spoke up. "How are we going to control this thing?" she asked. "We can't just follow Sykes around and wait until he pulls the trigger, as he put it."

Stone shook his head. "When the trigger is pulled, Sykes will be far away and in enough company to give him an iron-clad alibi."

"He'll believe he's not even a suspect," Tom said. "He doesn't know he's being listened to."

"Nobody is addressing my question," Claire said. "How are we going to control this?"

"I think," Bill said, "we have to offer Sykes an opportunity he can't afford to miss. Then we control the opportunity."

Holly spoke for the first time in a while. "I think by 'opportunity' you mean me as bait."

Bill shook his head. "I won't allow that," he said. "We just have to make Sykes, and maybe Eugene, **think** that you're the bait."

"We've anticipated this situation," Tom said, "in that, having learned from our dummy in the White House, we've been looking for someone who can **appear** to be you, ma'am."

"And I won't allow that," Holly said. "I'm not going to have some agent or, worse, some innocent risk dying in my place."

Nobody spoke for a while. Finally, Stone did. "Well, I believe that leaves us at an impasse," he said. "Bill won't allow you to be bait, and you won't allow anyone else to be."

"It's late," Tom said. "I think we should all sleep on this."

There was a murmur of agreement, and they each got to their feet and shuffled off to their quarters.

Holly turned off the bathroom light and came to bed, crawling, naked, under the covers with Stone.

"I've missed you," he said.

"Same here, pal. Of course, we don't get this plan right, **everybody** is going to miss me."

"You do understand," Stone said to her, "that whatever the opportunity is, you're going to be the bait. I don't see how you can avoid it, short of never leaving this house."

Holly sighed. "Yes, I know."

"All sorts of people have used doubles: Churchill, Eisenhower, et cetera."

"And what happened to the doubles?"

"They all died in their beds, as far as I know. Field Marshal Montgomery's double, having been an unknown actor, became a famous actor."

"Yes, I saw that movie when I was a little girl. Ham took me to see it."

"I don't think you'd be putting a double into real jeopardy."

"Why not? Look what happened to the dummy."

"The person would be armored up," Stone pointed out, "not a sitting duck like the dummy."

"'Sitting duck.' That has such a nice ring to it."

"And anyway, our side now has a distinct advantage: we've got two spies in the enemy camp and his hotel suite is bugged, both audio and video."

"Now that's the most encouraging thing I've heard tonight," Holly said.

"How encouraging?"

"All right. I'll agree to the double, if they can find one."

"Enough talk," Stone said, pulling her to him.

"Yes, yes."

49

Bess was having breakfast in her room in her nightgown and a robe when there was a knock on the door. She answered it, and Sykes was standing there. She let him in and closed the door. "Good morning." She went back to her breakfast and motioned him to take a chair at the table. "What's up?"

"I have some reconnoitering to do today," he said. "Why don't you do some shopping? I'm buying." He laid a black American Express card on the table.

"There's no limit on that card, is there?"

"There's a limit on the user," he replied.

"Better tell me now," she said. "It will be too late when I'm at Bloomingdale's."

"All right, five grand."

Her eyebrows went up. "Are we attending a ball?"

"You never know," he said, getting up. "I'll see you back here in time for dinner. I may have some news then."

"Let yourself out, will you?" she said, spearing a sausage.

He did so.

She waited awhile then unlocked the door to the adjoining room and rapped on it.

Fisk stood there in his pajamas.

"Are those Bureau-issued?" she asked.

"Come in."

"No, you come in. Sykes has just left to do some reconnoitering, as he put it."

"We didn't hear anything on the wire," he said, looking alarmed.

"Relax. I don't wear pearls with my nightgown. Anyway, that's all he said. Oh, he also said he'd see me for dinner. And he gave me his Amex card and put a five-thousand-dollar limit on my spending."

"Are you attending a ball?"

"That was my response, too."

"And what was his answer?"

"He said, 'You never know.'"

"What do you think that means?"

"I think it means he doesn't have a venue for an assassination yet. But I suspect he has a means of getting intelligence on that."

"Why do you think that?"

"Just a hunch."

"But he won't be shooting before dinnertime."

"Maybe not," she replied, "but who knows?"

Fisk got a call on his cell phone, which he took from his pajama pocket. "Yes? Good. Stay on him, but be careful." He hung up. "Sykes just left the hotel. We're following."

"Good, now get lost. I have to shower and dress."

Fisk left, and she showered and dressed.

As she was about to leave her room, Fisk came back. "I see you've been wearing a cheap wristwatch," he said. "I brought you a Rolex."

"What does it do?"

"It tells time. It also performs the tasks the pearls did. Just press the stem once to turn it on and again to turn it off."

"Got it," she said, slipping it on. Then she left and headed off to Bloomingdale's.

Holly sat at the head of the worktable and read through her schedule. "Excuse me for a moment," she said to the gathered group. She went into her office and motioned for Bill Wright to follow.

He had a copy of the schedule in his hand. "Do you see what I see on this?"

"I see two opportunities," she said. "St. Mary's College, where I'm giving an award to a theatrical group, and the Army Intelligence Center, in New Jersey, where I'm giving a speech to the graduating class. I think Jersey looks best."

"Maybe," Bill replied. "Sykes and his people already have uniforms, so they can blend in out there. On the other hand, security is tight at that center, so making an escape after the fact could be a problem."

"Which do you think?"

"I want to send people to both and thoroughly check them out."

"I'll look forward to your decision," Holly said. "Now, I have to get back to work."

Bill left, and Holly returned to the long table. "This is approved," she said, waving the schedule. "What's next?"

Bess was in a dressing room at Bloomingdale's, trying on a dress, when there was a rap on the door.

"Yes?" she said, expecting a saleslady.

The door opened a crack. "Are you decent?" a male voice asked.

"Tom? Come in."

Tom Blake walked into the booth, looking embarrassed. "Excuse me, but I need to speak to you about Sykes."

"All right." She turned her back to him. "Zip me up, will you?"

Tom zipped her up. "This morning, did you tell Fisk everything Sykes said to you?"

"Yes, I think so. Sykes wasn't there long. Why do you ask?"

"We've lost him," Tom said.

"Have you got people at the Army Intelligence Center and at St. Mary's?"

"Not yet; we were supposed to follow him wherever he went."

"Well, since we suspect him to use one of those two places, you'd better cover both, hadn't you?"

"I've requested more people from New York's FBI station."

"Do you expect they'll honor your request?"

"Yes, but they can be slow."

"I'm sorry, Tom, but my next problem is which dress to buy. You're on your own."

Tom made to leave.

"Oh, one other thing," she said. "Does Sykes have anyone following me?"

"We haven't spotted anybody, but behave as though you're being tailed."

"In that case, you'd better not be seen leaving this dressing room, or I'll have to scream for security."

"Thanks for your help," Tom said.

"Anytime." She went back to trying on garments. She particularly liked the selection of silk blouses.

50

Wade Sykes sat in the rear seat of his SUV, wearing his class A uniform, with his colonel's eagles on his shoulders, and waited for the traffic to move at the main gate of the Army Intelligence Center. The gate guards were looking closely at IDs and examining the trunks of visiting cars.

Eugene was at the wheel, also in his class A uniform, with its sergeant's stripes.

Finally, they pulled to a stop at the guardhouse. The sergeant on duty spotted the eagles and snapped off a salute, which Sykes returned. "Good morning, Colonel," the man said, peering into the car, which Eugene had taken care to clean of any items that might arouse suspicion. "IDs," he said. Eugene handed him both his and the colonel's, and the guard had a long look at them before handing them back. "Open the tailgate, please," the guard said. Eugene pressed the button. The guard lifted the floorboards and had a look at and around the spare tire, then closed the tailgate. He walked back to the driver's window and handed over the IDs. "Pass on," he said, and Eugene did so.

"The IDs held up," Eugene said.

"What did you expect?" the colonel asked. "They're the real thing. If they'd run them, our photos would have popped up."

"I guess we can't do better than that," Eugene replied.

Sykes consulted a map. "Second right," he said. "The auditorium will be on your left."

Eugene found the building and pulled into the parking lot, and both men got out.

Sykes walked to the main entrance of the building and tried the doors; they were unlocked. They passed through a large lobby area and the double doors. The empty rows of the auditorium lay before them. "It seats seven hundred fifty," Sykes said, "and I'm sure it will be full."

"Can we go upstairs?" Eugene asked.

The colonel led the way. "It has a projection booth."

The booth was in the center of the last row of balcony seats. Eugene tried the door. "Locked." He took a lockpick kit from his pocket and made quick work of getting inside. He did not turn on the lights but used a penlight. "I like this," he said, climbing into the single seat where the projectionist could watch the movie. He looked down at the stage, then opened the small viewing window. "Ideal," he said.

"That's what you said about the projection room at St. Mary's," the colonel reminded him.

"They're both ideal," Eugene said. "Our uniforms and IDs give us an advantage here."

"We'd have different uniforms at St. Mary's, but egress is the problem at both venues," Sykes said. "Let's have a look."

Eugene had a last look around, then the two men followed the EXIT signs to a door that opened onto an outside landing and a flight of stairs to the ground.

"Both front and rear entrances," Eugene said. "A piece of cake."

"Okay, then how do we get off the base?" the colonel asked.

Eugene pointed past the rear exit and across the

street. "Officers club," he said, "noncom club next door. I'll drop you at the first then park in front of the second. We can have a sandwich at the bar, wait for the hubbub to die down, then leave by the main gate, where they checked us in."

"I like it," Sykes said.

"So do I," Eugene replied. "But I like St. Mary's, too. I'd be wearing a workman's coveralls there. I can put the disassembled rifle in my tool kit, then walk outside onto a busy Manhattan street and get into the van. But here is different. How are we going to get the rifle on and off the base? I don't want to leave it. It's a fine piece of equipment."

"There's room under the rear seat," Sykes said. "I'll ride in the rear seat, like today, so I'll be sitting on the case."

"And we have the advantage of already being in their computer, both today and tomorrow. Nothing strange about us."

"Do you consider them both doable?"

"I do," Eugene replied.

"Equally so?"

Eugene thought about it. "It's a shorter shot at St. Mary's, but given the steep incline of the seating area, more downhill; but I can deal with that. Yes, equally so."

"Then let's go back to the city and think on it," Sykes replied.

They took the George Washington Bridge back across the Hudson River, because Sykes always felt trapped in a tunnel, even one as large as the Lincoln.

Bess left Bloomingdale's and couldn't find a vacant cab anywhere, so she hoofed it back to the Lowell, which was only a few blocks. Tom Blake was sitting in the hotel lobby, reading a newspaper. He did not look at her as she passed.

She was putting away the plunder of the day when there was a rap on the inside door. She opened it, and Tom was standing there.

"We've got a problem," Tom said.

"Come in and have a seat."

Tom sat down. "We've narrowed their opportunity to two venues," he said. "She's giving an award at St. Mary's College at nine AM tomorrow, then she's moving to the Army Intelligence Center in New Jersey, for an 1:30 PM event."

"So what's the problem?"

"We don't know which one they're going to make the attempt at."

"Jesus, Tom, then cover both of them!"

"We don't have the personnel. The president is in town for an appearance downtown tomorrow, and the White House has drained away all available personnel from both the Bureau and the Secret Service."

"How about the New Jersey State police?"

"They can't operate on a federal installation."

"Army MPs can."

"They're all tied up dealing with the traffic and visitors for the event."

"Have you got enough people to cover one event?"

"Yes, but barely."

"Then pick one and cancel the other."

"Peregrine refuses to cancel either, says they're very important to statements she wants to make—on the arts at St. Mary's and on national defense in New Jersey. Do you think you can find out from Sykes which one he's going to hit?"

"I think the odds are heavily against it. He's beginning to trust me, but we're not there yet."

"Then I'll call Stone Barrington. Maybe she'll listen to him."

"Now **that's** an idea."

51

Stone listened patiently to Tom Blake and Bill Wright on a conference call, then listened to all of the suggestions Bess had made. "So you're at an impasse again," Stone said. "And you're both afraid to insist that Holly make the choice."

Silence.

"Asked and answered," Stone said.

"Stone," Bill said, "we'd be very grateful if you'll speak to Holly on our behalf and get her to make the choice."

Stone sighed heavily. "And why do you think that will make a difference?"

"Because she's known you a long time, and she respects your advice."

"Is flattery all you've got, Bill?"

"It is."

"All right, I'll have a go. I'll wait until she gets home and put it to her then."

"She's not going to be home until around five o'clock, and she might get delayed beyond that. Please call her and speak to her now."

"Oh, all right. If she'll speak to me. She could be in a meeting."

"Please try."

Stone hung up and called Holly's cell phone.

She picked up immediately. "You're calling for Tom Blake and Bill Wright, aren't you?"

"Yes, but . . ."

She hung up.

Stone stared at the telephone, swearing at it. He called back.

"They have my answer," she said.

"No, they don't, because the question has changed."

"The hell it has."

"The circumstances have changed, too."

"All right, take your best shot, then I'll hang up again."

"This is your choice. If you won't choose one venue, then the Bureau and the Secret Service will cancel both of them."

"What?"

"You heard me; what's it going to be?"

"They don't have the authority to cancel those events."

"You're not president yet, remember? They can cancel them, and there isn't a thing you can do about it."

"That's outrageous!"

"No, it's not. It's sensible. What's outrageous is your insistence on doing both events, when you've been told they don't have the manpower to cover both."

"I don't believe them."

"They've explained it to me, and I believe them. Do you want me to explain it to you again?"

"What's my excuse for canceling?"

"Flu-like symptoms; you forgot to get a flu shot."

"I did so get my flu shot!"

"It isn't one hundred percent effective," he pointed out.

She thought about it. "If I say that, then it will start a whole big immunization thing, and I'll find myself arguing with all those people who won't let their kids be vaccinated for whatever."

"All right, what we need is a reason for your absence that isn't a lie."

"Tell me one."

"How about diarrhea and vomiting?"

"Too unattractive, and still a lie."

"Intestinal difficulties."

"Same thing."

"Exhaustion."

"Well, I'm certainly getting tired of talking about this."

"How about the FBI and the Secret Service made you do it."

"Which one?"

"Both of them?"

"Reason?"

"Because the president is in town for four events, and they're spread too thin to cover everything."

"Well, that has the attraction of being true."

"Can you hang on a minute?" He didn't wait for an answer, just called Tom Blake.

"Is Bill with you?"

"Yes."

"How about postponing both events for a day. Can you cover both the day after tomorrow?"

"Yes!"

"Hang on." He sent back to Holly. "We've got it, it's true, and it works."

"What does?"

"Postponing both events for a day."

"Oh, hell, all right. But they're making the phone calls, not I."

"Done." Stone hung up. "You still there?"

Both of them said, "Yes."

"Postpone until the day after tomorrow, and you two have to make the calls. Flip a coin."

"Great idea!" Tom said. "We'll confirm!"

"And Tom, Bill?"

"Yes?"

"If that doesn't work, reschedule them for different days, maybe next week, and clear it with the transition team."

"Okay."

Stone put down the phone and pondered the thought that it could be like this for the next eight years.

Shortly after five, Holly walked into his study, grabbed a bourbon bottle, got some ice, and poured. "You're in big trouble," she said.

"Bourbon, please," Stone said, looking up from the TV.

A CNN anchorperson came on. "It seems that events scheduled for tomorrow by both the president and the president-elect have overstretched the limits of protection that can be provided for

323

them, so the president-elect's events at St. Mary's College and the Army Intelligence Center, in New Jersey, have had to be canceled and rescheduled for another time."

"I guess the president takes precedence," his coanchor added.

Stone switched off the TV. "There, that wasn't so bad," he said.

"It wasn't, but you're still in trouble."

"Why?"

"Because neither event could be rescheduled before January 20."

"That is my fault, how?"

"Well . . ."

"Look at it this way: you don't have to go to New Jersey tomorrow and drive back during rush hour."

She sat down and kissed him. "Maybe you're not in such big trouble after all."

52

Bess, watching the local news, learned that both of Holly Barker's events had been canceled. Shortly, Sykes called and invited her for a drink at 6:30, dinner to follow. She appeared on time, wearing her new little black dress and her pearls.

When Sykes opened the door, Bess saw Eugene having a drink but, thankfully, he was not dressed for dinner. The TV was on, and Sykes went to turn it off.

"Can you leave it on?" Bess asked. "I like Lester Holt."

"Of course." He made her a drink and sat down next to his own. "How was your shopping day?" he asked.

"Just about perfect," she said. "I bought this dress, some trousers, and some silk blouses." She handed the Amex card to him. "Thank you." She squeezed an earring and turned on the pearls.

Lester Holt came on, read a couple of national stories, then said that Holly Barker's events had been canceled for the next day and why.

"Well," Eugene said, "that's one decision you don't have to make, Colonel."

"I guess we'll have to pick a new event when her next schedule is made up. We may be in New York for a few more days."

"Just out of curiosity," Eugene said, "which event did you decide on?"

"The one in New Jersey," Sykes replied. "We're both more comfortable in that environment than at an artsy-fartsy college."

"So true," Eugene said.

"What sort of event do you need?" Bess asked.

"Something like the two that were canceled. One will turn up, don't worry. She's a politician, she can't hole up for long. She's got to be seen and see people. She's already running for reelection."

"How can I help?" Bess asked.

"By enjoying yourself while you're in the big city," Sykes replied. "If we need you for something, I'll let you know."

"She needs to leave the transition office now and then, if only to go home for the night," Eugene said.

"She's staying at the Carlyle, which is on East Seventy-sixth Street. That block is congested because of the hotel entrance, and it's not good for us. I believe you and the boys have tickets to see the Knicks play tonight?"

"Right you are." Eugene stood up. "I'd better get going."

"Should we move on, too?" Bess asked.

"Our table's not until eight o'clock, and we have another guest coming for drinks."

"Anybody I know?"

"We'll see."

Bess was immediately nervous. What if it really was somebody she knew, or who knew her? There was a knock on the door.

Sykes opened it to admit a room-service waiter with a tray of canapés. He put them on the coffee table, accepted a tip, and left.

They watched another couple of minutes of news, and there came another knock.

Sykes got up and heartily greeted a man at the door. "Bess," he said, "this is United States senator Les Hardy," he said. "Les, this is Bess Potts."

Hardy, a tall, well-tailored man, greeted her

with charm and compliments on her dress and pearls.

"Thank you, Senator," she replied.

"Please, it's Les. I'm only just getting used to the title."

Bess recalled that the senior senator from Virginia had died a few weeks before, and that the governor had appointed Hardy, who only recently had been sworn in, to the vacant seat.

They finished a couple of drinks and left the hotel for dinner.

"Where are we dining?" Bess asked.

"At La Goulue, just down the street. We'll walk."

Fisk and Tom Blake listened to the transmitted conversation. "Well, there's a wild card for you," Tom said. "I had no idea that Sykes and Hardy were tight."

Fisk did a little work on Google. "They were classmates at West Point," he said, "and room-mates their senior year." He scrolled down. "Their paths crossed on a couple of assignments, too: one in Germany and one in Florida."

"What did Hardy do as a civilian?"

"He retired from the Army last year as a colonel,

and became a part-time lobbyist for a gun manu-
facturer. The Army was a big customer, and he
was a big contributor to the governor."

"Does he have any ties to any right-wing organizations?" Tom asked.

Fisk checked. "Only ones listed are a club in
Washington and the NRA."

La Goulue was crowded and noisy. Bess
wondered how that was going to affect the performance of her wire. There was nothing she could
do about it, except lean in for conversation, so she
decided to relax and listen.

"Pity about those schedule changes," Hardy
said to Sykes, after they had ordered dinner.

"We'll have other chances," Sykes said, "as long
as your friend keeps the information flowing."

God, Bess thought. I hope my colleagues
heard **that**.

Tom Blake and Fisk were listening intently on
earphones.

"Did you understand that?" Tom asked.

"I heard it, but I'm not sure I understood it,"
Fisk replied. "What information?"

"About Barker's schedule, I think. Can you
clean up some of the crowd noise on this audio?"

"No, but we've got a guy who can. I'll call him."
He picked up a phone.

A half hour later, a technician was at work on
the tape, while Blake and Fisk continued to listen
to the live feed.

"I think they regard that line as a slip," Fisk
said, "and now they've become more guarded."

The tech took off his headset. "You want to
hear it?"

Everybody gathered around the speaker.

"We'll have other chances, as long as your
friend keeps the information flowing."

"That's Sykes's voice, speaking to Senator
Hardy," the tech said. "Looks like he said what
you thought he said."

"Oh, shit," Tom replied.

53

Tom Blake, Bill Wright, and Stone Barrington sat at Stone's dining room table and listened to the playback, before and after the tech had tweaked it. Holly had had a dinner to go to and could not be with them.

"How do you read that, Stone?" Wright asked.

"I read it as Hardy has a plant on Holly's transition staff who's feeding them her schedule."

"I don't know how else anybody could read it," Tom said.

"Sam Meriwether is running the transition team. How much does he know about those people?" Stone asked.

"I haven't spoken to him yet, but they've

all applied for top secret security clearances. I've already asked our New York office to pull all applications and investigate them thoroughly."

"How long have they had the applications?"

"Only a few days. Target date for completion is January 2."

"Has anybody got a cell number for Sam Meriwether?"

"I have," Wright said.

"Give him a call and put it on speaker," Stone said.

Bill did so, and the vice president–elect answered immediately.

"Sam, it's Bill Wright."

"Evening, Bill, what can I do for you?"

"I'm with Tom Blake and Stone Barrington. Stone has a question or two for you, and we're all on the call."

"Hello, Sam."

"Hi, Stone. What do you need to know?"

"Tom has reason to suspect that there might be a leak from someone on the transition staff."

"A leak to whom?"

"To a person unfriendly to Holly."

"What's the nature of the leak?"

"Holly's daily schedule."

"I manage that, and I know most of our schedulers pretty well."

"Think about it: Is there someone among the schedulers that you might trust a bit less than the others?"

"Let me tell you how this works," Sam said. "We get a call—sometimes from a fund-raiser or other friend of the campaign—someone who wants Holly to speak or hand out diplomas at a graduation, or just to shake some hands. The call is directed to the scheduling team, and the person taking the call fills out a form taking down all the details: date, time, location, purpose of the gathering, numbers expected, like that."

"Go on."

"If that staffer thinks the caller isn't who he says he is, or that the event isn't worthy of Holly's time, she puts the form into an out tray and it comes to me. I decide if I think the scheduler is wrong, that it is an important event, and order it to be put on the schedule. If I agree that it's weak, a form letter goes out, over my signature, politely declining the invitation."

"What happens if the scheduler thinks it's a worthy event?"

"Then it goes to a scheduling supervisor, and if she thinks it's worthy, then it's discussed at a meeting, where we either schedule it or write a declining letter over Holly's signature, with a handwritten note at the bottom."

333

STUART WOODS

"So who sees the final schedule?"

"All the heads of the various subcommittees of the transition, at a daily meeting."

"How far ahead of the event?"

"As little as a day or two or any time before January 20. After that, the White House staff takes over."

"So how many people have knowledge of the schedule?"

"A dozen or fifteen."

"Have they all applied for a top secret security clearance?"

"Yes, every one of them."

"Have any of the clearances been granted yet?"

"No, the Bureau doesn't do it piecemeal. We'll eventually get a letter with a list of the cleared personnel. If someone doesn't make the cut, I'll get a phone call about why."

"Anybody turned down yet?"

"No."

"Sam, back to my original question: Is there anybody in that group that you trust a bit less than the others?"

"Anybody who used to be an extreme right-winger of any standing."

"What does 'of any standing' mean?"

"Someone who worked for somebody important at a level requiring trust."

"How many of those people are on the clearance list?"

"Well, there's one who used to be a press aide to a recently appointed Republican senator and one who was a policy aide to a Republican congressman." He gave their names, and Tom noted them.

"Anybody you have any personal qualms about, Sam?"

A long silence. "No. They're a good bunch."

"Sam, it's Tom Blake. A question . . ."

"Go ahead, Tom."

"Is there anyone among them who anybody thinks may have had ties with or even sympathy for a white-supremacy group?"

"No one that I know about, but a person like that wouldn't be broadcasting those views around here."

"Thank you, Sam. Anybody else have a question?"

Heads were shaken.

"That's all, Sam. Thanks for your help."

They said good night, then hung up.

"I'll give these names to the right people," Tom said.

"One other thing, Tom," Stone said.

"What's that?"

"I'd like to know if any of the people on that list are Virginians."

"Why?" Bill asked.

"Because we're dealing with a white supremacist from Virginia and, now, a senator from Virginia," Stone said.

"Fair enough," Bill said.

"Stone," Tom said, "have you spoken to Lance Cabot about his man on the inside, the cook, at Sykes's compound?"

"I confess I haven't, Tom," Stone replied. "I'll speak to him tomorrow morning."

"While you're at it, ask him to ask his man if he knows of any outside visitors to the compound, people who aren't members of his group."

"I'll do that," Stone said, and they adjourned.

54

The following morning, Stone got Lance Cabot on the phone, and they both scrambled.

"What can I do for you, Stone?"

"Talk to me about Leroy Collins, aka Elroy Hubbard."

"Are you a messenger from the FBI?"

"If you mean the assistant director you invited to lunch, then stiffed, yes. The question remains unanswered."

"Do you think we discuss our officers with just anyone?"

"No, and I didn't believe you would invite them to lunch, then stiff them, either."

"That was unfortunate. There was a flap."

"What was the nature of the flap?"

"You don't have a need to know that," Lance replied.

"Tom Blake has a need to know anything that will keep Holly Barker alive. I should think, given your past association with her—and your future service—you'd be happy to help him."

"Do you want me to tell you everything about Leroy's work?"

"I'd rather you'd call Tom Blake and tell him."

"Almost nothing."

"Say again?"

"Almost nothing; that's what Leroy Collins knows about Wade Sykes and his merry band of hatemongers."

"How long has Leroy been on the assignment?"

"Four or five months."

"And he's learned nothing? I don't believe that."

"**Almost** nothing. He's learned the name of the FBI agent assigned to the group."

"Thank you. Tom Blake already knows that—he sent her there."

"What would you have expected him to learn, Stone?"

"Oh, let's see. Has he learned that the junior senator from Virginia, Les Hardy, has visited the compound?"

Lance took a beat before he responded. "I beg your pardon?"

"I spoke clearly, Lance. Does that name surprise you?"

"I've heard it before."

"From Leroy Collins?"

"Not necessarily."

"Lance, who's running Leroy?"

Lance let out a deep sigh. "I am."

Stone doubted that. "Doesn't Leroy ever call? Don't you have heart-to-hearts?"

"Only when he has something to report," Lance said.

"Did you hear that Holly canceled two events yesterday?"

"Yes, something about the president being in the city and taking up all the oxygen, I believe."

"Did you know that Wade Sykes and one of his minions reconnoitered both sites the day before yesterday? Or that they learned about the visits from Les Hardy, who is running a leaker on Holly's transition team?"

"Where does your information come from?"

"From Tom Blake's agent, who wears a wire and picked up a conversation between Hardy and Sykes."

"If that information became any more widely known, it would threaten the life of my agent."

"No. Sykes never speaks about anything important when Elroy is around, because Elroy is black, and Sykes doesn't trust anyone black."

"That would account for Elroy's lack of productivity," Lance said.

"Lance," Stone said, "if I were you I'd find a way to make Elroy more productive or else get him out of there before Sykes twigs and puts the man in an unmarked grave."

"That's good advice, Stone," Lance said, "and I'll take it. Good day to you." He hung up.

Stone called Tom Blake.

"Yes, Stone?"

"I just spoke to Lance. He maintains that his agent has learned nothing, except that your agent is FBI. I suggested that he find a way to get more out of him or pull him out before Sykes kills him."

"I think that was good advice, Stone. Do you think Lance will do it?"

"Which one? Productivity or death?"

"I don't know how you make a mole more productive, do you?"

"No. I doubt that Lance does, either."

"So he'll get him out?" Tom asked.

"If he does, your girl will know about it."

"Maybe I should get her out, too."

"Why? It seems to me that she's been very productive."

"Because I don't want to get her killed."

"It's a little late for that. After all, it was you who sent her into that nest of vipers. Besides, if you pull her now, Sykes is going to take a great interest in where she went—and if he finds out, he'll kill her. He might even drop his plans for our lady, and if he does that, you'll still have nothing on him, and he'll go right on operating. And you haven't even started to explore where Senator Hardy stands in all of this."

"Actually, I have. We're turning over every stone as we speak."

"Anything on the transition team leak?"

"There are two people, a woman and a man, who have right-wing connections and hail from Virginia. Soon, we'll have a chat with them."

"May I make a suggestion, Tom?"

"Sure."

"Let me have that chat with them, separately. They will feel less fearful of talking with me, rather than with an FBI agent."

"Good suggestion, Stone. I'll mention it to the director, who is taking an interest in this."

"One other suggestion, Tom. I think Lance Cabot is going to yank Leroy Collins. If he does, you should press Lance to let you talk to Leroy. He might know something he doesn't know he knows."

"You're a fount of good ideas, Stone. We'll see what happens."

"One more," Stone said. "Before you talk to your two suspects on the transition team, think about setting up another stop on the schedule that resembles the two you canceled, but a fake. Maybe you can suck Sykes into making his move. Of course, you'll want Holly out of the way when that happens."

"I'll talk with Bill Wright about it," Tom said.

The two men said goodbye and hung up.

55

Holly sat at the common table at her headquarters and looked at her watch. She stood up and shouted to the room, "Everybody, be quiet and listen!"

The place fell silent.

"I've noticed of late how haggard you are all looking, and I can see that I've been working you too hard."

There were murmured denials.

"Don't lie to me," Holly said, "you're all exhausted. I want you all, every man and woman of you, to get up from your seats, take your coats, if you have them, and your personal effects, then go home."

Nobody moved. They just looked at her, stunned.

"Your specific orders are to go to wherever you sleep, order in a pizza and a cheap bottle of wine, eat and drink yourself into a stupor, then go to bed and sleep for twelve hours. That is all. Get out of here!"

They moved fast, before she could change her mind.

When Holly was alone, she went into her office, found a bottle of bourbon in a bottom drawer, grabbed some paper cups, went back to the common table, and sat down.

A lone woman appeared at the other end of the room and stood there, silently.

"Holy shit," Holly said to herself, unbelievingly. Finally, she took a deep breath and held the bourbon bottle aloft. "Come and have a drink," she said. She watched the woman approach. She looked eerily familiar. So did the suit she was wearing.

"Have a seat," Holly said.

The woman sat down.

"Who are you?" Holly asked.

"My name is Holly Barker," the woman replied. "I'm the president-elect of the United States."

"Well," Holly said, pouring them both a drink. "You've certainly convinced me."

They both raised their cups and drank.

"Where on earth did they find you?" Holly asked.

"I'm an agent at the DEA," the woman replied. "I've worked some cases with the Bureau, and somebody there remembered me. They got a hairdresser and a makeup artist in and burgled your house for this suit and a couple of others, then they dyed my dirty-blond hair auburn. I think I'll keep it this way."

"What was your name before you were me?" Holly asked.

"Geraldine Mason. Gerry, to you and everybody else."

"Did they tell you what they expect you to do?"

"I gather I'm to get myself shot, but not in the head. I'm wearing a vest under the suit."

"My nose is bigger than yours," Holly said. "Do you think you can pass?"

"People see me get out of the right car, and they'll believe what they expect to see."

Tom Blake, Bill Wright, Claire Dunn, Sam Meriwether, and Stone Barrington filed into the room and sat down at the table.

"Good job," Holly said. "She fooled me." She shoved the bourbon and cups down the table, and they all partook.

Tom Blake spoke up. "Here's how it's going to go down," he said. He spoke for five minutes or so, then stopped. "Well?"

"I think Holly, here, can pull it off," Holly said. "I hope the rest of you can, for her sake." She took a tug on the bourbon. "I've already forgotten everything you've told me."

"That's as it should be," Claire said. "We've had a chat with two of your scheduling staff. They'll be returning to work tomorrow, and they'll get a schedule that includes a thirty-minute stop at a theater at Hunter College, over on Lexington Avenue. It will be the only venue on your schedule that might work for them."

"Why do you think that?"

"It has steeply raked seats with a projection booth at the top. There's a fire door that exits to the street behind the college, where a parked van won't be noticed."

"Also," Bill said, "we have it on good authority that they're getting itchy for action, so they'll be more likely to bite."

"Did the cancellation of my two events this week have anything to do with them?"

"Yes. We were not only short of personnel, we were short on time to prepare. And we didn't have Gerry ready."

"Do you have time to prepare for this one?"

"We have already done so. We'll be ready for them at the scheduled time: eleven AM, the day after tomorrow."

"Where will I be when this is happening?" Holly asked.

"Somewhere else," Stone said. "You get to sleep late, if you like."

"What are the chances that Gerry here will get out of this alive?"

"As close to one hundred percent as possible," Bill said. "That's all we can tell you now. We need to keep some things from you."

"Do you consider me a possible leak?"

"We consider you a teapot," Claire said. "If you're too full and too hot, you might blow."

"And you want my approval?" Holly asked.

"They already have approval," Stone said, "they don't need yours."

"Why did you want me to send everybody home?" Holly asked.

"We have some electrical work to do here," Tom said. "Audio and visual. When they come in tomorrow morning, the schedule will be on everyone's desk. You can tell them that you and Sam worked out the schedule tonight."

Claire took a stack of papers from a briefcase

and started distributing the pages to the desks. Everybody else began to leave, except two Secret Service agents at the far end of the room.

Stone came to Holly's chair. "We can go now. How about some dinner?"

"I'm hungry enough to eat an ox," Holly said, standing.

"I don't think that's on the menu at Caravaggio," he said, "but they have just about everything else, plus the advantage of being right around the corner."

"Then why aren't we already there?" Holly asked.

He helped her into her coat, then offered his arm. "Right this way."

They walked down Madison to Seventy-fourth Street and took a right. As they walked into the restaurant and were escorted to their table, there was a sudden dip in the other guests' conversation.

"I'm having to get used to that," Holly said.

56

Bess was having lunch with Sykes in his suite when Eugene knocked, then let himself in and handed a sheet of paper to Sykes. "I believe we're on," he said.

Sykes looked at the paper. "Have you already reconnoitered?" he asked.

"No, but I found some photographs of the theater on their website, and a map check shows a street behind it where the van won't attract attention. We should get over there and check it out as soon as possible."

"I'll meet you downstairs in twenty minutes," Sykes replied.

"I'll let the others know what the van has to look like," Eugene said, then left.

"You look excited," Bess said.

"I am," Sykes replied. "When both our earlier choices got canceled, I thought they were on to us, but this place seems ideal."

"Where is it?" Bess asked. She was wearing her pearls.

"At Hunter College, over on Lexington." He went and got a New York City street map. "Here," he said, tapping. "And the van will be on the street behind. You'll be driving."

She smiled. "You're sure you can trust me?"

"Of course," he replied. "And if you fail us, we can always shoot you."

Bess just smiled again. "I won't fail you."

"Let me have your iPhone," he said.

She handed it to him.

"Let's go."

Down the hall a couple of doors, Fisk twiddled with some knobs. "We got all of that," he said.

"Is anything going on in that theater right now?" Tom asked.

Fisk looked at the schedule. "No, it should be empty. We finished our work there yesterday. All we had to do was tap into the college's own security network. We've got cameras and audio. You want to watch?"

"And record," Tom said. "We'll call it a cold run-through."

Sykes, Eugene, and Bess parked the van on the back street and walked up the fire stairs. Eugene had the lock picked in a moment, and he peered into the theater. "The lighting is dim," he said, stepping inside and holding the door for them.

They walked into a theater with maybe six hundred seats, lit by a single bulb from a work lamp onstage. Sykes found a bank of switches and turned on the other lights. "Follow me."

He led them across the front row of seats and up some stairs to another door behind the stage. He opened it to reveal a sitting room. "Here's their greenroom," he said. "She has a 10:30 meeting with the president, two floors up, so they're likely to take the elevator down and enter through the main door. They'll be briefly exposed on their way to the greenroom."

He walked them up the rows of seats to the projection booth. "It isn't even locked," he said, opening the door.

They walked in and looked around, then Sykes went to the projectionist's viewing window and sat down. "So you can get a first shot as she comes through the door."

"Maybe, but not ideal," Eugene said. "She'll likely be surrounded by other people. According to the instructions on her schedule, she's due to be in there by 10:45. That's when the main doors will be opened and the students and faculty will start to file in. When they're all seated, the curtains will be drawn to reveal the set for the play they're doing that evening, and the president will introduce her from the center-stage microphone. She'll enter from the greenroom at stage left, and when she's alone at the microphone, that's when I'll fire. When she's down and dead, I'll cut the lights from that panel by the door"—he pointed—"and we'll step outside and leave through the fire door on this level. Our two guys will cover us and shoot anybody who tries to follow."

"Bess, that's when you'll be on. The van's engine should be running, and as soon as the door is closed, you'll start down the street at a very normal pace, then turn two lefts onto Lexington and head downtown. We'll park the van in midtown and just walk away. It will have already been wiped clean, and everybody will be wearing cotton gloves, which we'll ditch at convenient trash baskets on the streets."

"Wade," she said, "we shouldn't ditch them anywhere near the van. They'll search every trash can for blocks, and if they find even one pair, they'll get DNA from them. When we get back uptown, we can douse them with something flammable and dump them there to burn."

"You're right, that makes more sense," he said. "Eugene, anything else to cover?"

"They're working on what we need for the van now," he replied. "The outside will read 'New York Video and Audio.'"

"We should rip that off as soon as possible. If somebody sees us drive away, they'll note the name," Bess said.

Wade looked at her fondly. "We may keep you on here," he said.

W e've got it all," Fisk said. "They're toast."

"First of all, they'll be toast when they're toast, and not before. Second, be goddamned sure that nobody shoots Bess."

"She will be in the van, remember?" Fisk replied.

"Then nobody shoots at the van at any time, until she is out of it and clear. Pass that order around; don't miss anybody."

"I understand," Fisk said.

The whole group sat at Stone's dining table early that evening and heard Tom Blake's report. "I've made sure that everyone understands not to fire on the van until our agent is clear of it."

"Why do they want her to drive?" Stone asked. "Are they short of hands?"

"She drove on the mission to kill Ms. Barker in her home, and Sykes thinks she did well. She's been pestering him, at discreet moments, to trust her and give her more to do."

"I see. It bothers me that she's on this mission in any capacity. Is that necessary?"

"It bothers me, too," Tom said, "but Sykes thinks she's necessary, so we can't pull her."

"If she's left alone in the van," Stone said, "just have her drive away without them, ditch the van, and beat it to transition headquarters."

"I'm certainly good with that, if she's left alone. If Sykes leaves somebody with her, she can't drive away until he's aboard."

"All right," Bill said. "Stone, I think that's the best we can do."

Stone looked at Holly, and she nodded. "Agreed," he said.

57

Elizabeth was lying in bed, in the semi-darkness, eyes wide open, reviewing the coming day, nailing down every detail, when there was a short rap on the connecting door. She had been half expecting it and had left the door unlocked. "Come," she said.

Tom Blake came in and found the only light to be from a large-digit electric clock on the bedside table. He could see her, up on one elbow.

"Come in," she said, moving over and leaving him room to sit on the bed.

He joined her. "I just want to see if you're feeling ready for tomorrow."

"More than ready; I'm excited," she replied. She brushed a lock of hair off her forehead, and a

355

nightgown strap slipped off her shoulder, making for an enticing view of her breast. "Don't worry about me," she said, putting a hand on his cheek. "I've rehearsed every detail, over and over."

"A new order. If you're left alone in the van, drive away. Don't wait for them. But not if someone is left there with you. I don't want to lose a good agent." He indicated the door with a nod of the head. "I've got to get back in there," he said. "I've got to be in that room, and alone." He walked to the door. Before he closed it, he said, "Good luck tomorrow. Take care of yourself, because you'll be on your own."

"Don't worry about me," she said, and he closed the door.

Five minutes after Tom was back in the room, his phone rang. "Blake."

"It's Stone Barrington. Any developments?"

"None. We're primed and ready to go. Is Holly worried?"

"No, she's tougher than I," Stone said. "She's dead to the world. I doubt if I'll sleep tonight."

"Relax, Stone. We're at a point where that's all we can do."

"Holly said something like that," Stone replied.

"She was right. See you in the morning." They said good night and hung up.

Stone was at the transition office at 8:30 AM; it would be the command headquarters for the operation. Tom Blake and Bill Wright were sitting in Holly's glassed-in office with a woman. Wright waved Stone in.

"Good morning, Stone," Bill said. "This is Betty Cromwell, one of our scheduling staff."

"How are you?" Stone said, offering her his hand. Hers was ice cold and clammy.

"Betty here worked for then state senator Hardy, of Virginia, in his Richmond office, before she joined us."

Stone got the message. He pulled up a chair and kept his mouth shut.

"So, Betty," Bill said, "as I was asking, how did you come to work for Senator Hardy?"

"A family friend knew him from the Army," she replied, "and I interned in his state senate office when I was just out of school."

"And how did you come to work for Holly Barker?"

"I was attracted to her ideas."

"Which ideas, specifically?" Bill asked.

"Defense, infrastructure."

"How about abortion?"

Betty blinked. "She and I have different views on that subject."

Bill consulted a file in his hand. "I see you attended a Pentecostal church."

"Yes. Isn't that all right?"

"Of course it is. I just wondered how a Pentecostal could work for someone who is so strongly pro-choice?"

She shrugged. "We can't all agree on everything."

"Who was your family friend who knew Senator Hardy?"

"Ah, I don't remember. I didn't know him well."

"Would his name have been Sykes?"

"Possibly. I don't remember."

"Did you ever visit Sykes's home?"

"Once, I think, with my father."

"What was your impression of his place?"

"It was very nice."

"Did you visit his library?"

"Yes."

"Did you see any books there that you had read before?"

She was now clearly uncomfortable, shifting in her seat. "I have to get to work," she said.

"Not today," Bill said. "You're off today. We're just going to sit here for a while and talk about your relationship with Colonel Wade Sykes."

Tom rose and left the room, beckoning Stone to follow.

"She's the mole," he said. "Let's leave her to Bill. He's a gentler interrogator than I—he'll get her whole story." Tom led Stone to the rear of the offices, to a room he hadn't entered before. There were a half dozen video monitors and some audio equipment.

"We'll listen from here, and watch as much as we can cover."

They both took seats.

"Holly was still sound asleep when I left the house," Stone said. "I don't know how she does it."

"Did you get any rest?"

"Off and on. How about you?"

"I finally dozed off, middle of the night. I had the on-call duty."

"Where's the van?" Stone asked.

"We don't know yet. They'll pick up Sykes and my agent, Elizabeth, at their hotel. After that, the whole lot will soon be ours."

"I didn't ask last night," Stone said, "but the

theater is supposed to be filled by a student audience, isn't it?"

"It was," Tom replied. "But we made some changes in the schedule."

"Is anybody going to get hurt?" Stone asked.

"None of the students. Others will."

58

Tom Blake walked into a rear room at the transition headquarters and watched for a couple of minutes how a fine theatrical cosmetologist could turn Gerry Mason into Holly Barker. That done, a hairdresser sprayed water on her hair and blew it dry, placing soft curls in the places that Holly had them. One of Holly's suits hung on a nail in the wall nearby.

Tom took Gerry's hand. "How are you feeling?" he asked.

"Calm, but excited," she said. "Ready. I don't really have all that much to do. The Secret Service agents will push me in the right direction."

"Are you armed?"

"I brought a piece."

"Do you have a shoulder holster?"

"Yes."

"Wear it. You probably won't need it, but if you do, you should have it."

"Thank you, Tom, I will."

Tom checked his watch. "We'll load up in about fifteen minutes."

"I'll be ready."

Elizabeth put on her underwear and slacks, leaving off her blouse, then slipped on her lightweight, flesh-colored shoulder holster, got into the blouse and buttoned it, leaving the top button undone Someone looking for a gun would get the sight of cleavage instead. She slipped on a light leather jacket and zipped it up halfway. She picked up her Sig Sauer .380, pumped a round into the chamber, then popped the magazine and replaced the round, before reinserting the magazine. She slipped a spare magazine into her jacket pocket, then finally she put on her pearl necklace and earrings.

The hotel phone rang. "Yes?"

"Bess, it's Wade. You ready?"

"I am."

"Meet me downstairs in five minutes."

"Sure."

Wade hung up the phone in his suite. "All right, Eugene is in place at the theater, and Earl is already on-site. Jimmy, you're in the rear seat behind Bess, who will be driving. These are your instructions: If you see a threat of any kind, or anyone displaying a badge coming toward you, you are to shoot Bess in the head twice, before you deal with the threat."

Jimmy looked surprised. "Isn't she one of us?"

"Do you understand your instructions?"

"Yes, sir, I do."

"Are you fully capable of carrying them out?"

"I am, sir."

"Then let's go."

Bess was waiting beside the van when they came out of the hotel. She tugged at her right earring, then got into the driver's seat and adjusted the mirrors and the seat. She was looking into the rearview mirror when Jimmy got in behind her. She noticed that there were beads of sweat on his upper lip. A first-timer, like her, she reckoned.

Sykes got in beside her. "All right, let's go. Normal speed, don't blow the horn or do anything to attract attention."

Bess started the van, put the gear lever in D, and pulled out onto Madison Avenue, then turned east on East Sixty-fourth Street.

"Any questions, Bess?"

"Nope," she replied.

"Jimmy?"

"No, sir, none."

Stone walked out of the transition office with a half dozen people, among them Gerry Mason and Tom Blake. Tom directed him into the front passenger seat. An FBI agent was behind the wheel, his badge clipped to his outside suit breast pocket. They pulled away from the curb.

"Stone," Tom said, "are you armed?"

"Yes," Stone replied, "lightly so."

"You are not a policeman. Do you understand?"

"Wrong, Tom. I'm still carried on the NYPD roster as a detective first grade. My shield is on my belt; do you want me to display it?"

"Regardless of what your status is with the NYPD, this is a Bureau operation. Do you understand?"

"Of course," Stone said. "I'm under your command, Tom."

"Then this is your first order. When we walk into the building, you may accompany us, but you stop at the theater door. You are not to follow us into the theater until I order it. Is that clear?"

"As you wish, Tom; I'll wait outside the door."

"Good. You may display your shield when you do."

They were quiet for a moment.

"Stone," Tom said, "how is it you're still on the NYPD roster?"

"Our present mayor, who was commissioner of police at the time, made me a gift of the badge, promoted me to detective first, and put me on active duty until further notice. I've never had further notice."

"Extraordinary," Tom said.

"Perhaps so, but I can still participate in a bust."

"Not this one," Tom said.

"You've made that clear."

"You don't know the drill for the bust, and I don't have time to plant it in your skull."

"Understood. If someone armed comes out the door, do you want me to arrest him or shoot him?"

"The first person out of that door, after the bust begins, will be me, so hold your fire," Tom said.

The van stopped outside the main door of Hunter College.

"Everybody out," Tom said. "Normal pace, no rush. Stone, bring up the rear."

"Right."

Two more agents joined the group inside the door, and the unit moved across the main lobby toward a pair of double doors. Stone noted that they were both carrying long weapons under their raincoats. It wasn't raining, he thought, outside or inside. Why did they need long weapons in a small theater? Stone wondered. He wondered about something else. Who was going to speak? Surely Gerry could pass for Holly at a distance, but she couldn't speak in her place.

This whole business wasn't adding up for him. Something was wrong.

They reached the double doors and stopped.

"Everybody ready?" Tom asked.

There was a murmur of assent from the group. The man in front of Stone put his palm on top of Gerry's head.

Stone had never seen that before, unless shots had been fired. The door opened, and everyone started inside, except Stone. He hung his shield on his breast pocket, leaned against the door, facing the lobby, and waited.

59

Wade Sykes stood on the landing of the stairs outside the fire door, scanning the street for hostiles—vehicles or persons. Nothing bad had appeared. He looked down at the waiting van; he could see Bess at the wheel but not Jimmy, whose presence in the rear seat was obscured by the vehicle's roof.

He half regretted the order he had given Jimmy, but it was absolutely necessary, in the circumstances. He simply could not rely on someone who had not completely earned his trust. He hoped that all would go well, and that she would remain a part of his group. He would know very shortly.

Then, from inside the building, came a short burst of gunfire.

———

Stone heard the first burst from the other side of the theater, and had no wish to stick his head inside the door while weapons were firing. They were firing rapidly now, coming from more than one direction, he thought.

Tom Blake opened the door to the greenroom a crack so that he could see the stage. The armored podium that he had placed at front and center, the sort that covered the president on speaking occasions, sheltered a single man, who was looking his way.

Tom gave him the nod, and the man stood up, still mostly covered by the podium, and fired a burst into the window of the projectionist's booth in the balcony. Hopefully, Tom thought, that would do it. But it didn't do it.

Eugene, standing behind the projectionist's steel chair, reflexively ducked as the glass in the window shattered, and rounds ricocheted off the chair. He moved to one side of the seat so that he could get a look at the shooter, and, to his surprise, saw a head behind the podium. God help him, it was a setup. He returned fire.

———

Bess, at the wheel of the van, heard the gunfire, and so did Jimmy in the rear seat. She looked ahead and saw an armored police van pull into the street and block it. Then, in the rearview mirror, she saw Jimmy make a move, followed by an incredibly loud report and the appearance of a hole in the windshield, in line with where her head would have been if she had not, as a defense against the police van, let her ass slide off the seat and drop her onto the floor, while clawing at her pistol under her blouse. Another loud noise, and a large hole appeared in the back of her seat, scattering bits of upholstery everywhere.

She flipped off the safety of her Sig Sauer, rotated to the right, and snapped off two rounds through the gap between the two seats. One of them caused blood to spray on the head lining of the rear seat, and more was coming from a hole in Jimmy's right eyebrow. Pure luck, she thought, then fired another round into his forehead.

Sykes took in the police vehicle and the action in the van with a single glance. He ran down the stairs, opened the front passenger door, and slammed it behind him. Jimmy was dead in the rear seat, and Bess was climbing behind the wheel. "Reverse!" he yelled, then looked over his shoulder and saw a police car on Lexington Avenue partially blocking their way. The van had started to reverse.

Sykes grabbed the wheel and looked over his shoulder. "Full throttle!" he yelled, and she stomped on it while he steered.

The van struck the police car where he had aimed it, just forward of the rear bumper, and the car spun about ninety degrees. "Stop!" he yelled, and Bess did. "Now, drive!" She turned until they were pointed downtown on Lex, and got lucky with the changing of the traffic signals. She had gone ten blocks before she had to run a red.

"Hang a left on Fifty-seventh Street!" Sykes yelled, and she did. "Turn right on Second Avenue!" They would go with the traffic. "Left on Thirty-fourth Street! Keep your speed up!"

Bess followed orders. "Where are we headed?" she asked.

"East Side Heliport." He got out a phone and pressed a button. "Start your engine!" he said. "Request departure to the south!" He listened for a moment, then hung up. "With a little luck," he said, "we'll catch it just right."

Now rounds were coming through the front wall of the projection booth, and Eugene was on the floor, firing back at a point lower on the wall. He got to one knee and cracked open the door so that he could see the fire exit, then he flung himself at it, got it open, and ran out onto the landing, in time to see the van reverse, ram a cop car, then turn down Lexington. He was on his own.

He started down the stairs, his boots ringing on the steel steps, then caught a full burst from somewhere; he would never know where. He fell the rest of the way down the stairs and lay on his back, bleeding into the gutter.

Why aren't there any police cars?" Bess asked.

"Because it didn't go down the way they expected," Sykes replied. "Turn in there. The gate is open. Drive onto the ramp!"

She did exactly as he told her. A helicopter was sitting on the tarmac directly ahead of her, its rear door open, and she turned to avoid the rotor, then stopped. Sykes had opened her door and was pushing her out. "Into the chopper!" he said, and she dove for the door. He was on top of her. "Go!" he yelled, climbing off Bess and into a seat, grabbing a headset. "You know the routing," he said into the mic. "You know the routing!"

Bess pulled herself up onto the rear seat beside him and found another headset.

"Where are we going?" Bess asked.

"To Virginia," he said, "by a devious route." He got his phone out and began making calls.

When he was sure the firing had stopped, Stone popped the door and looked warily around. The fire door on the other side of the theater was open, and Tom Blake and a couple of others were standing there, looking down at the sidewalk.

"Where have you been?" a female voice asked.

He turned to find the ersatz Holly, a pistol in her hand, looking at him. "How did this go down?" he asked.

"There was a guy hidden in the bulletproof podium over there. At a signal from Tom, we started firing up there." She pointed with the pistol.

CHOPPY WATER

The projection booth was riddled with bullet holes, many of them large. "What was he using?"

"A heavy rifle with a long magazine. There was somebody in the booth, firing back."

"Who fired first?" Stone asked.

She paused, then said, "Impossible to say."

60

Bess felt airsick after a few minutes of sharp turns. She found a bag in the seat pocket in front of her and threw up in it.

"How are you feeling, Bess?" Sykes asked after a moment.

"I don't know," she said, "how do I look?"

"Sick," he said.

"I'm sick, but I'm getting better," she replied, then threw up again into the bag. Now she felt better. She settled back into her seat and loosened the belt a little.

"Now you look better," Sykes said.

"I'm better," she replied.

Sykes looked at his watch. "We're going to pick up a passenger in about an hour," he said.

CHOPPY WATER

"Where?"

"D.C. Well, not exactly D.C. College Park, Maryland."

Bess shook her head, leaned back, and closed her eyes. If he was going to shoot her, now would be a good time.

A half hour later she noticed they were much closer to the ground—perhaps no more than a hundred feet. She looked forward and saw a runway framed in the windshield. "College Park?" she asked.

"The world's oldest continuously operated airport," Sykes said. "Built for the Wright brothers in 1908."

The chopper slowed rapidly, then set down gently on the grass next to the runway. A tall man who looked familiar stood waiting, dressed in a military-style jumpsuit. The copilot got out and stowed his luggage in a rear compartment, while the man climbed in and sat across from Bess.

"Les Hardy," he said, offering his hand. "We've met before."

"Yes, we have, Senator."

The chopper lifted off, climbed a couple of hundred feet, and continued its journey.

Hardy found a headset. "What went wrong?" he asked, looking at Sykes.

"Just about everything," Sykes said. "They were lying in wait for us. Everybody is dead but Bess and me."

"That's not necessarily a bad thing," Hardy replied.

"In the circumstances, no," Sykes said. "Nobody left to interrogate. Nothing in their pockets, either; we traveled light."

"What's the plan now?" the senator asked.

"I'm going to pick up some things at the compound, burn some papers, then we'll head to Roanoke and meet an airplane there. Very early tomorrow morning we'll land in Caracas. Nobody can touch us there, even if they know where we are."

"Well, goodbye to the Senate," Hardy said.

"Les, we both know you weren't going to be reelected. It's hello to a new life. And when we feel like it, we can get back to work."

"How does that sit with you, Bess?" Hardy asked.

"First I've heard of it. But, as Wade says, 'in the circumstances,' I can't think of anywhere I'd rather be."

"We'll be comfortable," Sykes said. "I bought

a house there more than ten years ago, under a corporate name. It's fully staffed and provisioned, which is good. Food is hard to come by in Venezuela these days. There are a couple of cars in the garage; all we'll need are new cell phones."

"We'll just pop into the Apple Store, huh?" Bess asked.

"Don't worry about it."

"What am I supposed to do there?"

"Write that novel or screenplay you've been dreaming of?"

"Not likely."

"We can just drop you off at the compound, if you like, but before tomorrow, you'll be chatting with the FBI."

"If I choose that option, what would you like me to tell them?"

"Oh, you've been there since last weekend. You've no idea where I went or how long I plan to be gone."

Stone sat in a different helicopter, one with big letters on the side, reading FBI. Tom Blake sat next to him, on a satphone, which he hung up.

"Where are they?" Stone asked.

"We lost them over Maryland," Tom replied.

"Senator Hardy is MIA from his office. Best guess is, he took the underground train to the House side and got a ride from somebody."

"We know where they've gone, don't we?" Stone asked. "They can't be anywhere else."

"Agreed, and we're taking steps to be sure they don't think we know."

"So," Stone said, "are we going to take the compound, just the two of us?"

"We'll have backup on the ground, but I'm not sure we'll need it. All of Sykes's people we know about are dead."

"I hope he doesn't have more buddies than we know about. Any news of Elizabeth? Like, dead or alive?"

"She drove the van away, then got on the helicopter with him," Tom replied, "so we'll assume she's alive."

"Unless she involuntarily deplaned at altitude."

"Don't be a pessimist," Tom said.

61

The sun was low in the sky when the pilot broke the silence. "Twenty miles out," he said.

"Go silent," Tom Blake said.

There was a change in something, Stone thought. He took off his headset. "Weird," he said to Tom.

"Ain't it? If they're there, they'll get a lot less notice of our arrival. Chet," he said to the pilot, "get us down to a hundred feet off the deck, then circle the property from a mile out. Let's see what we can see."

"Gotcha," Chet replied, and began his descent.

From a mile out, Stone could see no vehicles parked in the area. It was dusk now, and there were no lights on in the house.

"Chet, take us back to the main road and drop us on the tarmac, then stand off a couple of miles, where you won't be noticed from the air, shut down and keep your radio on and your cell phone ready. If we come under fire, we may need to call in help, which is about five miles up the road. If you see incoming aircraft, call me on the phone."

"Gotcha," Chet said. He took them down to an altitude of two feet and hovered over the highway, while Stone and Tom grabbed their weapons and jumped out.

They were wearing SWAT suits and armor and carrying assault rifles and FBI-issue 9mm Berettas.

"Do you read me?" Tom said over the intercom.

"Loud and clear," Stone said.

Tom began jogging lightly up the dusty dirt road toward the house. It was a mile or so, and Stone was sweating when they got there. Tom held up a hand, got out his phone, and stuck it under one side of his helmet. He listened for a moment, then ended the call. "Helicopter traffic coming in from the northeast, five miles out."

"The barn," Stone said, and the two men trotted over to the building and tried the small door in the big door. It was unlocked, and they stepped inside. There was a single car parked in the barn, an older one.

Tom got on his phone again. "It's Blake; backup requested, suggest you land a mile off and come up the road. It'll be dark when you get here." He got an acknowledgment, then hung up. "We'll just roost here until the cavalry arrives," he said.

They watched through a crack as a helicopter set down in the large parking area. Two men and a woman hopped out and walked toward the house; the chopper sat, idling.

"Elizabeth is alive," Tom said. "This is obviously a short stop for them, so we may have to go to it before our people join us. There are only three of them, after all, and one of them is ours."

"Whenever you say," Stone said.

Lights began to come on in the house.

In my study," Sykes said. "The safe is in there."

"What's in the safe?" Hardy asked.

"Everything: rosters, safe houses; a law enforcement wet dream." He moved toward the safe and tapped in a digital code. A spin of the wheel, and it was open.

"Hand me that cardboard box, Bess," he said.

Bess had a hand under her blouse, when Les Hardy stepped in and grabbed her wrist. "Is there a weapon in there?"

"Yes," she said.

"Why would you need a weapon here?"

"I thought I heard something, like a distant chopper," she said.

Sykes walked over to her, ripped her blouse open, and removed the pistol.

"No chopper sounds," Hardy said.

Stone and Tom left the barn through a rear door and walked to another building, trying to keep the helicopter pilot's back to them. Tom ducked under the rotor, edged his way up the side of the aircraft, yanked open the pilot's door, and stuck his pistol inside. "Freeze," he said. "Chop power now."

The pilot reached out, pulled the throttle to off, and flipped a couple of switches. The panel lights went off and the engine wound down. Tom unfastened the pilot's harness, pulled him from the chopper, and put him on the ground. A moment later he was handcuffed to the frame of the machine.

"Those in the house would have heard the

engine die," Stone said. "This is going to get harder now."

"I know," Tom said. "Judgment call."

Stone racked the slide of his rifle, pumping a round into the chamber.

You're a big disappoint to me, Bess," Sykes said. "I gave you chance after chance to gain my confidence, but you never quite made it." He put the pistol to her head and thumbed back the hammer. "Stand back, Les. You don't want to get all bloody."

The senator backed up a step or two, but not far enough.

A gun fired, and Sykes spun around as he took the bullet in the head. Hardy was spattered.

"You hold it right there," a deep voice said.

"You're not going to get an argument from me," Hardy said.

Elroy, the cook, stepped forward, relieved Hardy of his weapon, and put him on the floor, then he turned to Bess. "Do you remember how to handcuff somebody?" he asked, holding out a pair of cuffs.

"It'll come back to me," she said, accepting them. "And by the way, thank you for shooting

Sykes. I was going to do it myself, but that didn't work out." She handcuffed the senator.

"It was my pleasure," Elroy said.

"Everybody freeze!" a man shouted.

"Tom, is that you?" Bess said.

"It's me and Stone Barrington. Backup is on the way."

"You won't need it, there's just the two of us," Bess said. She pointed. "All that paper over there is everything you always wanted to know about Sykes and his coconspirators.

"And, gentlemen, meet Elroy Hubbard."

"It's Leroy Collins," Elroy said. "CIA."

"Lance Cabot sends his regards," Stone replied.

Then the sky was filled with rotor noise.

Stone let himself in through the front door of his house and entered the alarm code in the keypad.

"Who's there?" Holly asked over the intercom.

"Pizza delivery," Stone replied.

"Come on up, but it better be hot."

Stone headed upstairs.

END
January 31, 2020
Key West, Florida

AUTHOR'S NOTE

I am happy to hear from readers, but you should know that if you write to me in care of my publisher, three to six months will pass before I receive your letter, and when it finally arrives it will be one among many, and I will not be able to reply.

However, if you have access to the Internet, you may visit my website at www.stuartwoods.com, where there is a button for sending me e-mail. So far, I have been able to reply to all my e-mail, and I will continue to try to do so.

If you send me an e-mail and do not receive a reply, it is probably because you are among an alarming number of people who have entered their e-mail address incorrectly in their mail software. I have many of my replies returned as undeliverable.

Remember: e-mail, reply; snail mail, no reply.

When you e-mail, please do not send attachments, as I never open these. They can take twenty minutes to download, and they often contain viruses.

Please do not place me on your mailing lists for funny stories, prayers, political causes, charitable fund-raising, petitions, or sentimental claptrap. I get enough of that from people I already know. Generally speaking, when I get e-mail addressed to a large number of people, I immediately delete it without reading it.

Please do not send me your ideas for a book, as I have a policy of writing only what I myself invent. If you send me story ideas, I will immediately delete them without reading them. If you have a good idea for a book, write it yourself, but I will not be able to advise you on how to get it published. Buy a copy of **Writer's Market** at any bookstore; that will tell you how.

Anyone with a request concerning events or appearances may e-mail it to me or send it to: Putnam Publicity Department, Penguin Random House LLC, 1745 Broadway, New York, NY 10019.

AUTHOR'S NOTE

Those ambitious folk who wish to buy film, dramatic, or television rights to my books should contact Matthew Snyder, Creative Artists Agency, 2000 Avenue of the Stars, Los Angeles, CA 90067.

Those who wish to make offers for rights of a literary nature should contact Anne Sibbald, Janklow & Nesbit, 285 Madison Ave, New York, NY 10017. (Note: This is not an invitation for you to send her your manuscript or to solicit her to be your agent.)

If you want to know if I will be signing books in your city, please visit my website, www.stuartwoods.com, where the tour schedule will be published a month or so in advance. If you wish me to do a book signing in your locality, ask your favorite bookseller to contact his Penguin representative or the Penguin publicity department with the request.

If you find typographical or editorial errors in my book and feel an irresistible urge to tell someone, please write to Sara Minnich at Penguin's address above. Do not e-mail your discoveries to me, as I will already have learned about them from others.

A list of my published works appears in the front of this book and on my website. All the novels are still in print in paperback and can

AUTHOR'S NOTE

be found at or ordered from any bookstore. If you wish to obtain hardcover copies of earlier novels or of the two nonfiction books, a good used-book store or one of the online bookstores can help you find them. Otherwise, you will have to go to a great many garage sales.

ABOUT THE AUTHOR

STUART WOODS is the author of more than eighty novels. He is a native of Georgia and began his writing career in the advertising industry. **Chiefs**, his debut in 1981, won the Edgar Award. An avid sailor and pilot, Woods lives in Key West, Mount Desert Island, and Santa Fe.

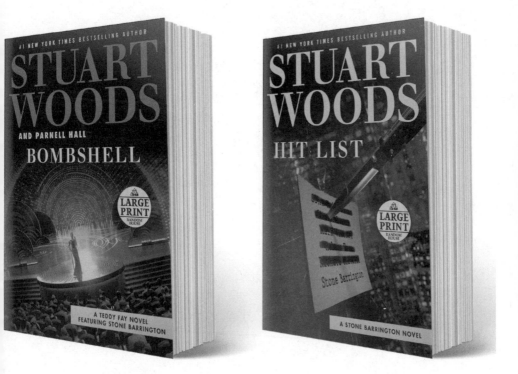